# Shadow Bands

# Shadow Bands

stories by
Jeanne Schinto

Ontario Review Press / Princeton

Most of these stories have previously appeared, sometimes in a slightly altered form, in the following journals: "Sounds of the Rude World" in *Four Quarters*; "Caddies' Day," "The Eel Man" (as "The Boathouse"), and "The Ring: Or, A Girl Confesses" in *The Greensboro Review*; "Before Sewing One Must Cut" in *New England Review/Bread Loaf Quarterly*; "The Friendships of Girls Unpopular Together," "The Motorcycle Riders," "The Original Dog," and "Shadow Bands" in *Ontario Review*; and "The Disappearance" in *The Yale Review*.

Cover art: "Cutglass Sea" by Alice Neel, courtesy Robert Miller Gallery
Cover design: GK&D Communications, Inc.

Publication of this book was made possible in part by a grant from the National Endowment for the Arts.

**Library of Congress Cataloging-in-Publication Data**

Schinto, Jeanne, 1951–
    Shadow bands: stories / by Jeanne Schinto.
        p.    cm.
    Contents: Caddies' day—The original dog—The friendships of girls unpopular together—The ring, or, A girl confesses—Before sewing one must cut—The eel man—Keepsake—Sounds of the rude world—The motorcycle riders—From a juror's notebook—The disappearance—Shadow bands.
    ISBN 0-86538-065-1 (pbk.) : $9.95
    I. Title.
PS3569.C498S54   1988
813'.54—dc19                          88-19830
                                                    CIP

Ontario Review Press
in association with Persea Books

Distributed by George Braziller, Inc.
60 Madison Ave., New York, NY 10010

For my husband, Bob

# CONTENTS

# Shadow Bands

# Caddies' Day

T HE BOTTLE IS STICKY around the spout. Do not pick it up by its spout. Keep your hands far away from the spout. A caddy's mouth has germs.

Two brown ants run around the rim of it. The caddy who threw it left a sip. Maybe the golfer was calling him to come on along. So he flung it beyond the caddy path, and it would have broken if he hit a rock. Behind those rocks caddies hide their bicycles. Caddies steal from one another.

I don't often walk along this path during the day. I come out here after supper. The golf course is empty of everyone then, but not sounds: the sprinklers tick around. And I take the flag out of its hole and march and sing. Sometimes I drop the flag and run because the darkness falls so soon. I run and climb the chain-link fence behind our house without cutting open my hand. My sneaker toes fit into the fence holes exactly. In a year or two they'll be too big. I do not tear open my hand, because I'm careful.

My mother thinks I am walking home the other way. On the road. I usually do. But today I have dirty paw prints down the front of my new dress, and I'm sneaking. I'd like to sneak into the house the cellar way so my mother won't see me and scream. Maybe I can take my dress off outside and bury it under the leaf pile in the corner of the back yard. If my mother says why don't you wear that little party dress Aunt Rhoda gave you anymore, I'll say I will next time, next time. And then I'll think of it rotting. And if she looks for it in my bedroom closet and doesn't find it and asks me where it is, I will say I don't know, it's not in there? It's not? And I'll start to look for it too.

The path is dusty, the color of a dog. The dust rises up. Over the bunker, on the green, the grass is short. Short as hair. As short as the milkman's. He told my mother: I don't even have to comb it when I get out of bed in the morning. Lucky duck! Sometimes the milkman pinches my cheek. It hurts. I give him a look. Then my mother gives me a slap. What'sa matter? He's saying he likes you.

On the green, a golfer is down on his knees, with his cheek to the grass. He's looking to see which way it's growing. My father said. He doesn't play golf, but he knows the greenskeeper, Mike, and Mike knows plenty. He runs the machines and he's very tall and dark, with a smile like an open tractor shovel. He talks to policemen all the time, and in summer, he has a crew of boys working for him. Members' sons, my father says, and this makes him shake his head and look sorry.

Change falls from the golfer's pocket. Nobody sees it but me. Not the golfer and not the other three with him. If the golfers had caddies, the caddies would see, but they have carts instead. And after they are going up the fairway, I scramble over the bunker. I pick up the coins—there are three—quarters, so big and round and silver. They looked funny lying on the grass. After the coins are in my pocket, the men look back and see me and wag their fingers. These are the two of them who are walking. The other two have driven the carts far up the fairway. And they say no, you better not play here, little girl. A ball could come and knock you on the head. Dangerous. Someone will hurt you, little girl. And don't be walking on that green.

Back on the path, I think, that's what they always say, and a ball hasn't hit me yet. I'd like to see them try and hit me with such a tiny ball. I'd go up on the fairway and stand. And I'd bet them, and I'd win. If I saw the ball coming close, I would duck and they wouldn't see me. They would be too far away. And

God would forgive me. He wouldn't want me to be killed. He loves me and watches out for me and knows the number of hairs on my head. He sees everything. And if I pulled one out by the roots? He'd see, even if he was busy. Even if he was busy saving someone from drowning. I would not be killed. Heaven is scary.

I see the caddy shed. From here it looks like a shoebox. And I hear the caddies' voices. They are swearing, but do not be afraid.

I'm not afraid, but I stop to read each tree. They are carved deep with initials, names, and hearts with arrows through them. My mother says that will kill the poor trees, gouging out bark with knives, and where do those boys get knives anyway? My father says the letters will grow, stretch right along with the bark. I'd like to see that. And I'd like to carve my initials here, but I don't have a knife. Some night after supper, I'll take one from the drawer in the kitchen.

The caddies' voices get louder as I walk along. It sounds like they are having a fight. Maybe they won't see me, and I'll sneak past them like a ghost. They'll be too busy spitting, shouting, shoving each other. On Caddies' Day they play golf themselves, and I hide behind the bunker and watch. They have fights, spit their words, raise their clubs. In the fall the bunkers burn. I used to think the caddies did it, and I cried. Our house would be burned. Then I saw Mike, the greenskeeper, with his torch. Fires burn black right to the path.

Not all of the caddies are young. Some of them are men my father's age, but they do not look like him. They look like his friends, the ones my mother says are vulgar. I do not see them yet. They are on the other side of the caddy shed, but I can hear them and I can picture them. They sit on two long wooden benches, their backs up against the shed. Unless they are playing cards, and then the benches face each other. Their shirts have wet marks under the arms. Hair curls around their ears. They smoke, hold their cigarettes between their teeth when they have to throw a card down. Sometimes they take the cigarettes from their mouths and call out to me. Comeer, little girlie. Sit on my lap, little girl. Other times they don't see me at all, and I walk the rest of the way home with my heart beating right out through my shirt.

And today? I think I will be safe! I will crawl past them unseen! They are all standing, shaking their fists, shouting, pointing to the benches. Both of the benches have been dragged out from their places up against the shed. One of the benches has been kicked over, legs up. Yes, I think, I will be safe! And I stride along. But then something happens.

A boy holding a card between his fingers swaggers to the center of the crowd. He wears a black T-shirt and his pants are too short and a curl of hair hangs in his eyes. He holds the card up, shows it, each side, as if it's a moth he's caught. He flicks it, watches it flutter down, turns and walks away.

Half of the caddies follow him, walking backwards and swearing at the others, who stay behind. Passing the fallen bench, they lift it high onto their shoulders. They walk with it to the carved trees and are about to set it down. But then the boy in the black T-shirt sees me.

He nudges the others, lifts his chin, looks behind him, smiles. I smile, too, a little. Then he takes the bench up himself, lifts it over his head, walks to the path with it, and sets it down across it.

The fence runs the length of the path. It runs all around the golf course. I could climb it right here and then walk home on the road. I would go in the kitchen-door way, and my mother would see my dirty dress, and I don't care. But the caddies all are watching me. They would watch me climb. They would see my underpants. They would see if I fell. And if I cut my hand on the twists of wire at the top of the fence? I wouldn't want to run to them and ask them to make it stop bleeding.

Besides, on the road there are dogs I'm afraid of. They are not like the dog at the party. One of them bit me, a tiny dog, no bigger than a cat. But its teeth were like a rat's. It was a Chihuahua. My mother told me a dog can smell fear, and I must have had the smell on me that day. My father said next time give it a good kick in the teeth. Should I? A dog that small. God wouldn't like it. One of his creatures. They all have their purpose. What should I do?

I could go around them on the other side, on the golf course grass. The golfers would scream, but I would explain. They would give me time. Then they would come back to the caddy shed and scream at the caddies. I've seen them scream at them before. Men with red faces, red pants, red shirts, potbellies like they're expecting. White belts around them, white shoes, little hats. My father calls them fairies. I ask him what do you mean? He laughs. My mother makes a smirk. Sometimes the golfers hit the caddies. Well, I saw that once. And when it rains, a storm, golfers don't share their umbrellas with the caddies. The golfer takes the bag and walks ahead and the caddy walks behind —or runs. Or stands under a tree. My father says that's one way to get his hair curled but good when the lightning strikes him. I watch them shivering under the trees. No wonder caddies are so mean.

One of them comes up to me. His shirt is striped, his pants cuffs drag, he is holding a bottle. His palm is flat to the bottom of it, one finger stops up the spout, and he tips the bottle sideways and watches the bright red soda slosh. I watch it too, and then I see there is something else inside. It is filled with tiny brown ants riding on the surface of the red. They make a ship inside the bottle, inch-high, climbing over one another. Below, some have sunken into the red and are drowning.

I look up into the caddy's sweaty face. He is as tall as a tree and smiling. One of his front teeth is chipped. All of his teeth are yellow and must have germs, but you can't see them. Germs are invisible. He says, "Hey, girlie, you gotta pay the toll," and he turns and points his chin back over his shoulder at the other caddies on the bench across the path. The one in the black T-shirt gets up and starts coming toward me. "Don't walk backwards," he says to me. "You might trip over something. A tree root. See those roots behind you?" He laughs and the one with the ants in the bottle laughs too.

And then I laugh. I cannot help it. I cannot stop the laugh. I try to make my eyes look mad, but they are laughing too. Sometimes when my father's friends tell a joke my mother tries to frown, but I can see her smiling, laughing behind her frown. Once I was kissing my doll and I could not stop that either.

I feel a tickle. The caddy in the black T-shirt is tickling my neck. Then he tries to brush the dirt from the front of my dress. And he straightens my bow. If he were my father or my mother

or my aunt, he would tell me to twirl and show him how far
the skirt goes out. Well, that was when I was smaller. But he
doesn't ask me to twirl. He is talking, like the other one did,
about the pay toll ahead.

He asks me if I have any money while the other caddies from
the bench gather around. I tell him no with a shrug. I shrug and
shrug to each question he asks, because that eases the tickle.
His hand is still tickling my neck.

He asks me, "What are you doing walking down the caddy
path anyway? This is for caddies only. Didn't you know that?
And nobody should leave the house without at least a couple
pieces of change. Didn't your mother even give you a dime for
a phone call in case you got lost? And how'd you get your dress
front all dirty?"

Sweat.

I sweat from my upper lip, from my forehead, my chest. I
like to feel the first sweat of summer. It happened in the
schoolyard this year. I was playing jump rope: high-water, low.
A girl everyone hates was holding the rope, and she tripped
me, and everyone sneered at that girl and came to see if I was
all right. With all of them standing around me in a circle, I started
to cry. I was not hurt very badly, no blood, but I knew they
wanted me to cry. I knew. They wanted to see me hurt good
enough to cry so they could make the other girl scared, feel bad,
worry that we would tell the teacher. And we did. And I cried
some more when she came over. I wonder if I should cry now.
Wonder if that is what the caddies want me to do.

"Hey, girlie, how 'bout a little kiss?"

I do not look into their faces. I look at their knees spread
wide. One of them has his hands out.

After supper my father puts his hand palm-up on the table,
and I'm supposed to put my hand inside it. And I do. This is
an old game. I'm too old now. But he makes me play. And I
do. And he says, "How much do you love me?" And I say, "Five
hundred." "How much?" He squeezes my hand. "A thousand."
"How much?" "Ten thousand!" "How much?" "A million!"
"That's better," he says. Then he lets go.

One of them puts a hand on my shoulder. It is heavy as an

iron. I used to not be able to pick up my mother's iron. She used to tell me to stay away from the board when she was ironing. Once, I was playing underneath it. That was my house. I was hiding. She was on the phone. When she walked back into the room and found me, she screamed.

They are whispering among themselves. Maybe I can walk away. My feet in my shoes are sweaty—they will squeak. But if my feet were bare they would make little footprints in the dust. And then the caddies would follow them right to the cellar door and up to my room.

Their voices are like low rumbles of thunder. I look up and watch the Adam's apple of the one with the bottle of ants. It looks as if it will soon burst through. It looks as if it hurts him. The hand on my shoulder is squeezing hard. It's the hand of the black T-shirt boy. Then it's lazy—resting, not holding. I start to walk away. Then I run. And a shout goes up. And everything changes.

My ankles hurt me. My nose hits their knees. I am upside down. They hold me by the ankles and laugh, thumbs pressed into my bones. Then money drops. Coins on the ground. They are dropping their money? No. It's the money I found on the green. I forgot about it.

"No money for the toll, huh? What's this? What's this?"

Someone picks up the coins. Snaps my underpants. I try to cover them with my dress. Someone takes my hands.

Sometimes I walk around my room with a mirror under my eyes. Everything is upside down. And I walk in the world upside down. I like to do this best when my room is messy and my mother says clean it up, it's a pigsty, clean it up now! And I take the mirror and instantly it's clean! The ceiling-floor so white and neat makes my room instantly picked up! I want my mother to look into the mirror with me, but she won't. I know without asking. Besides, there's only room for one pair of eyes at a time.

I want to cry. Will my mother hear me? I don't want my father to see. He would come and kill them with a steak knife from the kitchen drawer. I would stand behind him and plead: they don't mean any harm. Passing me from one to the other. It's a game. They are laughing. Hear them laugh! My ankles hurt, and my nose. But they don't know it. They think I like it. I am laughing, too. Sometimes when you squeeze my hand, it hurts, and I say nothing, I laugh. And you, mother, nod, and say that's a good girl, and you laugh. Look at their faces! What do you think? Maybe they're saying they like me.

Then they put me down.

My feet feel funny on the ground. I'm dizzy and do not walk away. They are waiting, watching me to see what I will do next. They look a little afraid. That is funny, too. I think they think I'm going to do something back to them. What could it be?

The boy in the black T-shirt whispers something to the one with the ants in the bottle and gives him a smack on the shoulder to send him on his way. The ant boy throws his bottle down—it doesn't break; it rolls—and he goes back to the caddy shed, hands in his pockets, head down. The rest of the caddies are all around me, watching and waiting still. There is an opening in the circle. I could walk out of it, but I don't—even though I know that they wouldn't stop me if I tried.

When the ant boy returns, he has a new bottle of soda. He hands it to the black T-shirt boy, who hands it to me. It's orange. My favorite. How did he know? The bottle is icy and clean. I want to put it to my cheek, but they are waiting for me to take a sip.

I take a small one. The black T-shirt boy says, "You're okay, right, girlie? Right?" And he's frowning, and I'm scared again, but I know what to do. I nod. And all of the caddies smile. And I smile, too, and sip again.

Two of the caddies sit down on the bench and start to deal the cards. A couple more go get sodas of their own and bring them back to the path and drink them. I am getting full, but I keep drinking, even when a golfer comes over. "Who's this? Who's this?" he asks. "What's going on?" But all of us keep drinking our sodas. We are celebrating something.

# The Original Dog

Sitting on the stoop with his two miserable dogs, old Franklin watched Dream Boy shuffle into the alley. The boy carried barbells, one in each hand, and was dressed like a boxer in plum satin shorts, no shirt, and bright white sneakers. Franklin ran a finger under his nose and stroked one of the dogs—small, nervous, wearing rhinestone collars—and he did not take his eyes off the boy.

He was about sixteen and small for his age, or thirteen and overgrown. His arms and legs were spidery, his chest concave, and his bush of kinky, cloud-colored hair made him look fragile, wispy, like a dandelion gone to seed. When the boy put the barbells down he turned to the one unbroken garage window in the alley's whole line, plucked a three-pronged comb from deep inside his bush, and began poking through to his scalp with it in furious little takes.

Franklin straightened and spoke to the dogs. "That's good— it's goddamn good to be strong, build yourself up. Boy couldn't defend himself now if he tried. 'Course if he works at it every day . . . But I bet he don't know a thing about weights."

One of the dogs was a Chihuahua the color of milky tea. Its eyes were large and frightened. The other was a long-haired dachshund that never sat but stood, constantly shifting its weight, as if it were ready to run at the first sign of danger. Still, the dachshund was the bolder of the two—it did not have to be carried out of the kitchen door, curling around Franklin's arm.

Dream Boy lived in a house across the alley from Franklin. It was brick, unpainted, with a chimney that seldom stopped smoking in winter. The boy's father was a black man, about fifty years old, who drove a dented blue station wagon. Every day the man backed the car up to the fence behind his house and hauled out of the back of it and into his yard whatever junk he had collected around the city—old TVs, tools, tires to sell, and scrapwood to burn in his fireplace when the weather turned cold. The man's name was Clothesline Sims. Before he started to deal in junk, Sims stripped clotheslines.

Franklin knew Sims. The old man had spent thirty-five years on the D.C. police force, walking the same blocks where Sims used to steal. For the last thirteen years, Franklin had been retired, and although he had heard that Sims was an honest man now, he never spoke to him.

Dream Boy stood straight, hands on hips. Then he dove, touched his palms flat to the ground, and bounced back up, hands on hips again. He did this thirty or forty times without stopping or even slowing down, with a motion that was fluid and continuous, like a skater's figure eight. But it was also brutal, violent, Franklin thought—as if Dream Boy meant to do himself harm, to turn himself to liquid and spill across the ground.

Since the summer began, Franklin had watched the boy act like the alley was his bedroom. In the morning, the boy would sing in a tormented falsetto as he punched the thick, humid air. Afternoons, he argued with himself in the glass of the garage window. At night, he often walked in wide circles in the beam of the alley's only street light, silvery moths fluttering above him.

Franklin was surprised he did not hate the boy. Instead, he discovered with some embarrassment, he could overlook the boy's flat, triangular nose, bee-stung lips, and the black man he had for a father, because he was fascinated by his skin: it was a stained ivory color, like old piano keys. And there was something else. Once, in the early part of the summer, from his kitchen window, Franklin saw the boy throw himself down between two garbage cans and cry, banging his head against the rough concrete. Franklin paced for a minute or two, clenching and unclenching his fists. Then he smiled, reached up and flipped the radio dial until he found some lilting music, turned up the volume, and pointed the radio out the window.

After that, Franklin began to engage Dream Boy in imaginary conversations that went on for hours. Today Franklin leaned forward slightly and began: "Did you get the notice? They're turnin' off the water from nine till noon tomorrow. After it goes back on I'll put the washer through its paces four or five times to clean everything out. After they get to workin' on those pipes down there they loosen up all kinds of impurities. The washer uses eighty, ninety gallons each cycle. Flushes all that stuff away. But I wouldn't do it for myself. My body's strong, nothing could get to it. I fuss with the goddamn water for the sake of the dogs.

"Did I tell you where I got them? A Richmond concern. Man by the name of Orville Mason is a breeder down there. Saw the ad for them on the day they took my wife to the hospital. They got here on the day she was buried. Made them a bed in one of her roastin' pans. Lined it with bath towels. She wouldn'ta liked that too well. They're pedigreed, though."

Franklin moved his lips when he spoke to Dream Boy, but the words were barely audible. It was as if he were reading aloud to himself or to a child almost sleeping. He did not move his lips when he told him his dreams, however. Those he simply rolled across his mind. Today Franklin chose the dream about the combination nursing-home/kennel. In that, Franklin was the proprietor of such a place. He wore a brown woolen suit, but it did not itch. His dogs, looking calm, even intelligent, sat on chairs at the front desk, a bluish fluorescent light shining down on their heads. The ladies and gentlemen who lived at the home, each with a pedigreed dog by his bed, sat up on their elbows and nodded gratefully as Franklin passed by in the hall.

"What do you make of all that?" Franklin asked Dream Boy, who had moved into the shade of a tall weed tree and was jogging in place, and then Franklin felt foolish. If the boy had even once noticed Franklin it was not apparent. He never said hello or smiled or raised his hand in greeting. He never even lifted his chin slightly, the gesture that risked the least.

Could be he's blind, Franklin thought facetiously. Then he decided it was better that their conversations were one-sided. It was safer. Franklin was in control.

The control was most important when Franklin ran the nightmares through his brain for Dream Boy. In the nightmare that Franklin recalled for him today, his wife, wearing her faded bathrobe, stood alongside the dining-room hutch, with its doors swung open. She was scowling and pointing into it, as if it were a brand-new icebox on the blink. His wife looked so real. Everything about her was clear, sharply defined. Even the tiny pink roses on her bathrobe. Franklin might have been looking at her through a pair of very strong glasses. Franklin walked over to the hutch and looked inside. The sight seemed to throw him several feet. His dogs were stuffed inside, like broken toys in a chest. "I told you that would happen," his wife said, wagging her finger at him. "You smothered them." Franklin opened his mouth to scream but no sound came out.

As if he heard a strange sound suddenly, Dream Boy cocked his head in Franklin's direction. Franklin straightened, and so did his dogs. But Dream Boy turned away again and picked up the barbells and raised them over his head. Slowly he moved his arms out to the sides and began to make wide circles. He faced the garage window for this and his eyes never wavered until a mutt wandered into the alley from the street.

The dog was colt-like—spindly and sleek. It trotted on three goods legs. It held the fourth up, folded into its side, and it kept its snout close to the ground.

Dream Boy called to the dog, making kissing sounds, but it trotted by him indifferently on its way to the line of overflowing garbage cans. Expertly the dog tipped over a can by leaning his body against it. Then he thrust his head and front paws inside it and began to feast, banging the can against the concrete.

With narrowed eyes Franklin watched the mutt. His dogs watched too, yapping wildly, but they did not leave the stoop. Franklin and his dogs seldom did, though it descended not into the alley directly but first into Franklin's small fenced yard. Franklin had trained the dogs to use a litter box in the pantry, and a white-haired black man from a few doors down came weekly in these warmer months to trim the grass and take care of the few scrawny rose bushes.

Previously, Franklin had not left the stoop because of his wife. Ill and laid out on a twin bed in the dining room, she might have called out to him, and in the yard he was out of earshot. Her voice was weak, like a cupboard closing, and Franklin did not hear so well either.

Franklin had cared for his wife in the dining room so her doctor, seventy-three himself, could quit climbing all those stairs to the bedroom. The doctor had complained about them repeatedly in his deceitful, good-natured way, always with the artificial smile, and Franklin had sensed that sooner or later he would have used the climb as an excuse to stop coming. But the dining room arrangement suited Franklin as well as the doctor. Franklin too had grown tired of the seventeen steps. He was tired of carrying her meals up, her bedpans down to the bathroom, of never being able to play the kitchen radio loud enough, of never stepping outside the kitchen door. He was always waiting for her call.

To Franklin, by that time, had come not just resentment but envy—the bitter desire to trade places with his wife. He began, in her presence, to speak of her in the third person. Suddenly he no longer cared whether she did or did not pass away that day. And with a careless, empty expression on his face, he picked up the phone and made plans to move her, as if she were a piece of furniture, to a more convenient spot. He ordered the bed from a department store downtown and set it up with the help of two delivery men. The men carried her down the stairs. For himself, Franklin dragged the living-room couch into the dining room. There he slept for the next five years. When she died, he took over the bed.

The mutt in the garbage can and Dream Boy with his barbells made Franklin think of the circus. A sad-faced clown and a circus dog. Once Franklin took his wife to the circus. They sat on the top row of the D.C. Armory bleachers on a hot August night. A colored girl with a green bow in her hair sat next to them, and at one point during the high trapeze act, the girl gasped, threw open her arms, and accidentally stuck her finger into his wife's gaping mouth. His wife insisted they leave immediately, so she could go home and wash out her mouth with vinegar and brown soap. Franklin found the whole thing comical, but was glad it had not happened to him.

But Franklin did not like to think about his wife anymore. He shifted his weight, patted the dogs, still yapping, and went on talking to Dream Boy: "Made a tin of corn bread this morning. You could have some. I could bring it out here if you didn't want to come inside. The dogs wouldn't bother you.

"It's so cool in the kitchen, so hot on the street. And dirty. This city, this neighborhood, so wild now—with whores and such paradin'. That bar on the corner, next to the funeral parlor. Used to be a real nice place. A restaurant where families gathered. Knew the man who owned it. Irish. Nice-lookin', but with freckles. Used to kid him about the freckles."

The mutt, having eaten his fill, moved toward Franklin's fence, wagging its black cigar tail. Franklin's dogs began to dance and yap even more wildly. Franklin got to his feet muttering, scooped up his pets into his arms and dumped them into the kitchen. Inside, the dogs kept on caterwauling, but Franklin ignored them and watched the mutt running back and forth behind the pickets. When the mutt began to howl back at the dogs inside, Franklin stood up and waved his arms and said, "Hee-ah! Hee-ah!" as if he were trying to get a stubborn horse to move. The mutt seemed to smile and shrug, then it trotted off on its three good legs.

When it was gone, Franklin slowly reseated himself and reached around behind him to crack open the screen door. His dogs, still wailing, tumbled out. The dachshund began chasing its tail and rolling its eyes. The Chihuahua threw itself against the curve of Franklin's spine, retreated, then rammed him again, and again. Franklin never once tried to appease them. Finally, exhausted, they settled back down into their flank positions beside him and began to pant, each with its tongue hanging out and flapping like the end of a cinched belt.

"Never used to be bothered so much by mutts," Franklin told Dream Boy, who was still lifting his weights, and had not so much as blinked in the direction of all the noise that Franklin's dogs had made. "Enough of 'em run through here. But then I heard something about them on the radio: If all the fancy breeds in the world were let loose and allowed to mate any which way, it wouldn't be long before there weren't nothin' but Original Dogs —'mongrels that roam the alleys of every city in the country.' I wrote a letter to the *Star* about all the damn mutts loose. Maybe they'll print it. Once, they printed another letter of mine: about the woman down at my old precinct substation who was eight-months pregnant and still on the job. No excuse for that. I wrote a goddamn good letter too. I'll read it to you. Got about ten copies in the house."

Franklin got up and went inside, his dogs following close by his heels. He was smiling broadly, Franklin was, even humming a little. Maybe he would really talk to Dream Boy today, hang his arms over the fence and gab. He could imagine Dream Boy's voice, thick and smooth, like honey being poured into coffee.

When Franklin returned to the stoop, however, Dream Boy was preparing to leave, stacking the weights as he slid them off the bars. At the same time, a girl from the street sauntered into the alley. She was black, with gingerbread-colored skin, she had an aimless look about her, and she was wearing a startling outfit. Her red shorts were so tight and cut so high her buttocks were partially squeezed out of them. A white frilly top showed her shoulders and midriff. On her feet were pink platform heels. She had blonde straw-like hair so stiff and straight it stuck out like points, and she had heavy make-up on her eyes. She was chewing gum and calling someone's name.

As Franklin watched her, his heart began to flutter. The boy, ready to leave, stopped to watch her too. Then the mutt with the three good legs careened around the corner. "There you are—you," the girl said to the mutt, who began to circle her. Twirling to keep her eye on the mutt, she caught sight of the boy. She forgot about the dog, put her hands on her hips, spread her feet apart, and smiled a wide smile. Franklin looked from her to the boy. He was smiling back at the girl. She beckoned the boy with a crooking finger. He inched over. They stood there in the alley talking, she slapping her palms on her thighs and laughing occasionally, he lacing his arms together and pulling them tight as if they were towels he was trying to wring.

The mutt lay down to watch on a shredded mattress in the shade. Franklin, watching too, began to sweat. It felt as if fleas were nibbling at his armpits. What would happen here? Dream Boy couldn't just go off and leave his weights in the alley. Someone would come along and take them and Franklin wouldn't stop them. No siree.

When they finally left the alley together, she pulling the boy by the hand, the mutt went back to the row of garbage cans; Franklin sat on the stoop numbly, his fists under his chin; and his dogs began to yap madly once more. The can the mutt toppled this time was more bent and jagged than the rest. The garbage men tossed them all like empty beer cans when they were finished dumping them. But the one the mutt was nuzzling in wasn't even owned by anyone. No one took it in after the garbage was collected. It just got filled up with the overloads of others, the soda bottles and other trash thrown by people passing through the alley. The can itself was trash. But how do you go about leaving a trash can for the men to take away? Franklin thought he could make a sign. "Take this too." But who said those jacklegs could read? Niggers. White trash. The city was filling up with garbage. Franklin could not even abide those new white couples, he realized suddenly and with a strange kind of pleasure. The men all rode motorcycles and wore beards like Jews. The women carried their babies in sacks that hung from their necks. The whole city was going to hell. And now Dream Boy . . .

"A whore, wouldn't you know," Franklin sneered. "And a whore's dog."

Suddenly, Franklin was up and off the stoop, on the grass—spongy, wet grass—at the fence, at the gate. He held the gate's padlock in his hand. It was like a cold heart. But he had the key for it in his pocket. Somewhere he had the key. He fumbled for it, found it, and opened the gate.

His dogs were still on the stoop, yelping, chasing their tails, rolling their eyes, wetting. Franklin ignored them and walked into the alley as if in a trance. He approached the mutt, still with its head in the garbage can. When he got within a few feet of it, the mutt jerked up and ran, circling, looking backwards at Franklin, who imagined that the mutt was actually laughing at him.

Franklin strode quickly to the barbells, lying on the ground. He picked them up, one in each hand. He would kill that mutt, he thought calmly, with the strength that he had built up over the years seeming to collect in his tightening fists. When he turned, though, he saw the mutt dance into his yard, and dance out again, shepherding his hysterical dogs out with him.

"No!" Franklin screamed. "Goddamn mutt! Suzie! Princess! Suzie!" He dropped the barbells and ran after them, as far as the edge of the alley, watching them run past the funeral parlor, the restaurant, and then around the corner. When they were out of sight, he stopped and walked slowly back into the alley and over to the old shredded mattress, a rain-soaked pile of rags, in the corner under a tree. He dropped to his knees, then onto his stomach, his face in his hands.

Suddenly he was more tired than he had ever been in his life. He had used up all his strength, it seemed, but not by running. Franklin started to cry. He amazed himself at the strange blubbering noises he could make, and after a while he was crying merely to hear the noises. The boy's weak too, he thought suddenly, as he fell into a dreamless sleep.

Hours passed. Franklin still had not moved. Then, the rumble of a car pulling into the alley

"Hey, old man," someone yelled out of the car window. "I got your dogs here." It was Clothesline Sims, returning with his day's haul of junk. Blinking, Franklin looked up and saw them, Sims in the front seat, the dogs in back, jumping up and panting, clawing at the car windows, which were shut tight. Franklin tried to struggle to his feet.

"Listen, old man." Sims got out of the car. He had long legs. He was wearing old baggy blue jeans and a light blue work shirt. He had a space between his two front teeth, just as Franklin remembered from so long ago on his police beat. "You need some help? What you doing out here on that raggedy old thing anyway, man? Come on." Sims held out a leathery hand.

"My dogs got loose. Goddamn whore's mutt chased 'em," Franklin said, taking Sim's hand. At the same time, Dream Boy sauntered back into the alley from the street, a pink towel hanging around his neck, his sneakers in his hand.

"Where you been, boy?" Sims asked him, as if he did not expect an answer, and the boy did not give him one, but started snapping the towel at him.

Franklin, standing there still holding onto Sims, was embarrassed. He shook loose. "I'm all right!" he shouted. "All right!"

"Okay, man," Sims said, his voice up an octave, his hands up, like a bandit's, and his eyes wide in fake fear. "Suit your stubborn old self." He opened the car door and Franklin's dogs tumbled out. "Goddamn little mutts. Shoulda let 'em get hit right out there in the middle of the street." Then Sims turned to the boy and said, "Hey, boy, gimme a hand here," pointing into the back of the station wagon where there sat an air conditioner and many long pieces of wood, four kitchen chairs with their seats punched out, and an ironing-board frame.

Franklin tried to meet Dream Boy's gaze as he passed him, but Dream Boy would not look at him. He was watching the dogs, who were simpering in circles, crouching down, expecting to get hit by Franklin, but Franklin was ignoring them. "Mutts," Dream Boy mumbled and laughed. Then he went around to the back of the station wagon and started to slide the air conditioner out.

Franklin looked at the boy fiercely, one last time, then he scooped up his dogs—they were so light: they felt like nothing—and he walked slowly back to the stoop, holding them tight, feeling his strength return, holding them tight and hoping to hurt them, hoping to break their useless little legs.

# The Friendships of Girls Unpopular Together

T HE FRIENDSHIPS OF GIRLS unpopular together are particularly sorry. One hopes for the best from these friendships, but it rarely comes.

I don't remember who my first pen pal was, but I do remember my last one. Her name was Mary Jane Dunphy and she lived in Bridgeport, Connecticut.

We were matched up as a service of the Beatles International Fan Club. I gave them various statistics about myself, and they gave me Mary Jane's address. In turn they gave her mine, but I was the first one to write. I waited and waited for a response. Ten days passed.

It was May, and at school we'd rehearsed all month for the procession to honor the Mother Mary. Early on the morning of her Flower Feast, I snipped an armful of purple bearded iris, ironed my pastel-colored dress, and walked uptown to the church.

The nuns roughly took us each by the shoulders, their black, berry-sized beads clicking as they worked, shoving boy, then girl, then boy into the long, hard golden oak pews. Some boys, in order to be kept still, needed an even greater separation from each other. In these rows were put two girls, then a boy, then two girls—handmaids of the most trustworthy kind, who rarely spoke or laughed with either gender; shy in and out of church. I was one.

While our straining voices blended, near the end of the first hymn, as always I saw Mary's statue smile, and I cried a little. I had grown worried throughout the month, because this statue was a new one—muted, putty-colored with vague, modern lines, unholy, unsentimental. Not like the old one, clad in blue and white, with realistic crimson lips and chaste, ivory teeth.

When the priest began to say the Mass, I prayed for the souls in Purgatory, particularly those who were there for impure thoughts and had at least a thousand years to go and had no one here on earth any longer to pray for them. By the time the first Communion bell rang, I felt I had earned myself a prayer: I asked for a letter from Mary Jane, and for a trip to Liverpool. The trip to England was the prize being offered to the winner of a Beatles jingle contest. A radio station in Boston was the sponsor. I had tuned in the station one clear night and heard the announcement from so many miles north; I told Mary that I understood that this was a sign, sure proof that God, her Son, Jesus Christ wanted me to enter, wanted me to help myself, wanted me to win. I had already sent in twenty postcards or more, finding among my stamp collection stamps that did not look cancelled, and affixing them to three-by-five cards.

We were given a half day off from school in order to go home and have lunch to break our long Communion fast, and there Mary Jane's letter sat on the kitchen counter! To "Miss" Estelle Otthouse! In a careful ink-pen script on sophisticated, bumpy blue stationery! The letter began with a short apology for having taken so long to write back. And then some talk about the Beatles, and her school, and her family. "You're Catholic, so you *couldn't* marry John, even if he *got* a divorce," she wrote in a postscript. I was forced to agree. I went upstairs and lay across my bed to write her a long response.

That summer I became a haunter of stationers. I visited my favorite one so often, the proprietor came to suspect me of something irregular. He assigned a clerk to watch and follow me every time I entered the store. I did not often buy paper—not as often as I would have liked to, anyway. Usually I just browsed, planning what I might buy if I ever had a pen pal who required a daily tome. Mary Jane, like the many others before her, was never as prompt a correspondent as I, and I resisted the impulse to write to her out of turn. What if our letters crossed? That would confuse everything. Besides, there was nothing for me to respond to, without a letter in hand. When I wanted to write blind and cold, I took down my diary.

It was Mary Jane's idea that we meet. Bridgeport wasn't too far away. I think now she was merely too lazy to write as the summer wore on. I asked so many questions, and perhaps she imagined that many of them might be answered with the proper facial expression instead of three or four paragraphs of her beautiful script. We exchanged school pictures, and I took the bus up to Bridgeport.

Flesh is so much realer than words, and Mary Jane had a lot of it. She was not fat; just very, very tall—perhaps even close to six feet; she loped camel-like towards me when we picked each other out of the crowd. She was smiling, and she had not been smiling in the school picture, so I could see her crooked teeth poking out from beneath her upper lip. I thought she should have told me about the teeth, just as she had about her height. I took it almost as a lie that she had not been smiling in the picture.

Girls such as I was do not shake hands, but Mary Jane did. She gave me a limp rag of a handshake, and bobbed her head down low to me in a kind of bowing gesture, half mock. Then she seemed unsure of where to put her gangling arms. She tried resting one on her hip, the other on top of her hat. She was wearing a black John Lennon cap as we had prearranged. I wore a madras Ringo cap, the better for her to recognize me. I was about to take the hat off—it made me feel foolish, even though I considered it almost a religious garment—but then came rushing towards us out of the newsstand a man as tall as, or taller than, Mary Jane: her father. Mr. Dunphy's hair was black and oily as the hair of boys at school, and was combed into a curl that hung down into his face. He kept thrusting it aside with a flip of his neck. He flipped and smiled, rushing towards me, he, too, with an outstretched palm. So I shook hands twice in two minutes, probably for the first time without jesting, without saying, "Shakespeare, kick in the rear!" and delivering the kick in the behind. Mr. Dunphy and I exchanged some niceties, he all the while surveying me very carefully—me, the little return addressee in the corner of my envelopes now come alive. Then he led the way to the car.

As we drove, Mr. Dunphy pointed out to me the murky sights of Bridgeport. Mary Jane and he were in the front seat; I sat in the back. Mr. Dunphy kept turning around to be sure to look at me while he spoke. I saw he was very much younger than my parents; he reminded me of boyfriends of my sister—overly polite and so sincere: I felt a little sorry for him and didn't know why. Mary Jane did not speak and seemed bored, and until she found a good song flipped the radio dial back and forth, which made a noise that to me sounded like someone falling down a flight of stairs.

Mrs. Dunphy, a lofty tree of a woman, met us at the kitchen door. She wore a white apron, and had lunch all ready: steaming bowls of chicken-noodle soup, slabs of homemade bread spread with butter softened just enough, and big wedges of homemade apple pie and speckled vanilla ice cream for dessert. We said no grace. Throughout the meal, Mr. Dunphy talked, while Mrs. Dunphy ran from stove to table, whispering softly, continually, like a big tree stirring, "Mary Jane, Mary Jane," with behavioral suggestions. I made a vow in my head at once that when I grew up and married a Beatle and had children I would be a mother exactly like Mrs. Dunphy, and my Beatle husband would be exactly like Mary Jane's father. He'd be living incognito of course as, possibly, a university administrator, which is what Mr. Dunphy was.

After lunch we went to Mary Jane's bedroom, a frilly, pink place.

"Do you want to see your letters?" she asked, looking around the room as if she could think of nothing else to do with me.

"Yes!" What a wonderful suggestion. "I always wish I could see where my envelopes end up, with the postmarks and everything."

"I didn't save the envelopes," Mary Jane mumbled as she reached a long arm underneath her bed and pulled out a shoebox.

"Oh, well," I said, hiding my disappointment. "My mother told me never to write in a letter what I wouldn't want printed in the newspaper. This way, with only the signature, they won't be able to trace me."

"Do you save my envelopes?" Mary Jane asked warily.

I nodded guiltily, wishing for once that I were able to bring myself to lie.

"Better get rid of them when you get home."

I said meekly that I would.

I read through a few of my letters, but grew uncomfortable. Reading them over was like catching a glimpse of myself in an unexpected mirror. This was me, each signature testified, but I still could not quite believe it. In my mind's eye I always pictured myself in my pastel-colored dress, looking pretty. These letters had been written by a lonely little girl. Had I really suggested to Mary Jane that we invite our favorite Beatles to the States? My plan was to have them over for the weekend, at her house or mine; we could cook them dinner, watch TV; on Sunday, take them to church. If that ended up in the newspaper, I'd die a thousand deaths, and go to Hell, for denying it—every single word.

Mary Jane's father drove us to the college stadium that evening. Mary Jane had gotten us tickets to a Herman's Hermits concert. She asked her father to leave us off quite a distance away from the main gate, so that we might walk in unassisted, so to speak, like the other young people moving along in great droves.

We sat in the bleachers between happy couples, who crawled over, under and around us to get to their seats, then out of their seats again, to visit with friends. Girls hung onto boys, kissing them, and vice versa. I saw Mary Jane alternately stare at the couples, then look embarrassedly away. How did one learn to kiss people? I had practiced on mirrors, but it hadn't instilled the kind of confidence I needed to actually try it. I squeezed my hands between my knees, very glum.

When Herman and his band ran rollicking out onto the field, my mood did not improve. The matchbox stage was so far away, I could not keep myself reminded that the boys were real. They reminded me of a trained flea circus I had seen once at a carnival. Also, I liked better the renditions of their songs that they had recorded. Whenever they deviated, to my ear, it sounded like a wrong note struck. And of course they weren't the Beatles. I had to be an appreciative guest, though. I didn't mention what I was thinking to Mary Jane, but I wished that the concert would soon be over, that the whole weekend would. Impulsively, I told myself I would not write to Mary Jane again.

When the concert ended, we walked to the spot where Mary Jane had told her father to pick us up. On the drive home, she flipped the radio dial as she had done on the way back from the bus station, and this time I was grateful for the noise. I could not hear what her father was saying in his cheery singsong voice, so I did not have to respond. He did not often ask a question, I noticed. He simply made observations that he himself found poignant or amusing. He had a way of smoothing over everything, making everything seem nice. Things weren't all nice—didn't he see? There were very many things which were bad. Should I point them out to him? The couples walking home together . . . ? Should I shout or start crying and surprise him? Him and Mary Jane both? I did nothing but sit quietly, picking out the sights of Bridgeport by myself, having begun to recognize them from the morning, even though now it was as dark as less nights can get. Besides, when Mary Jane turned her head, to catch a final glimpse of a couple walking arm-in-arm, I saw that she looked just the way I felt.

"Mary Jane, Mary Jane." Mrs. Dunphy shook our shoulders to awaken us. We dressed and ate toast and thick black raspberry jam for breakfast, and dragged ourselves to the car without speaking. Even Mr. Dunphy said nothing as all four of us drove to the home of Mr. Dunphy's boss at the university.

The Dean of Faculty, thin, pale, and timid as a balding third-grader, with a priest-like edge of authority to his small voice, made the towering Mr. Dunphy hunch. The Dean's wife, very big, sweetly scented, too sweetly for this early in the morning—like certain unpleasant flowers—commanded Mrs. Dunphy's attention with a piece of gossip that curled her lips as she delivered it. Then she and her husband got into the car.

The couple was about to embark on a transatlantic voyage. The Dunphys would see them off. I would be dropped off at home on their way back through my town, and none too soon. Mary Jane and I had had to squeeze into the station wagon's back compartment with the luggage, like a couple of children. Mary Jane, her legs folded foal-like under her, sulked heartily. Neither of us was any too happy about cuddling up with each other. After the concert, when we got home, we had started to sour and snap at each other. This morning, we slept, or pretended to, until we heard Mr. Dunphy cry out to God at the early-morning spectacle of New York harbor.

We parked the car and found the ship—it looked like the side of a building. It looked in no mood to be going anywhere, but would nonetheless in a few hours be wrenched from this side of the ocean and made to find its way to the other. I began to grow excited about this bon voyage. There was an excitement here. I felt somehow a part of this crowd, this time, moving towards the ship, speaking many languages. I hurried. I could hardly wait, for what I did not know. I looked to see if Mary Jane felt it, too, but I couldn't tell if she did. She was walking in her same loping steps. She seemed to have allied herself with her mother now; she walked along beside her, though her mother paid no attention to her. Mrs. Dunphy's job today was to listen to the boss's wife, her head turned slightly so that the Mrs. Dean might see Mrs. Dunphy's implacable grin as she listened enraptured. "I'm like one of those big ships myself now," the Dean's wife was saying. "I take a day to stop, a day to reverse direction, a day to get going in the opposite direction again."

The ship did not rock, at least we did not feel it, no more than we felt the movement of the earth spinning on its axis as we had long ago learned in school that it did. But the ship did tilt off at a definite angle, creating a fun-house effect that made me feel mildly reckless.

A steward showed us to a lower level. The sailors and other stewards we passed winked at us two girls. The young men all wore uniform hats and pants that made them look like schoolboys, innocent and slightly unreal—or like circus people, theatre types heading for the nearest stage. All of them seemed to have bright red lips, which looked painted.

A waiter brought a tray of canapes to the stateroom of the Dean and his wife. They were devoured, largely by me, while Mrs. Dunphy eyed me. Then Mr. Dunphy suggested we girls go take a look around the corridors of the ship by ourselves. The stateroom was after all no place for six, and perhaps he was just a little embarrassed by me. I had sat down on the Dean's bed, elbows back, swinging my legs.

Mary Jane had to be coaxed into going with me. She preferred to stay with the adults. I would have been just as happy to go exploring by myself. I was thinking of stowing away. Never mind the Beatles jingle contest. I would write to my parents when I got there. And to Mary Jane, too, I supposed, reneging on my vow to forget her.

The walls of the corridors were a dingy yellow—the color of nicotine-stained teeth—shined as best they could be, but dulled all the same. In our nostrils was the smell of frogs and toads and other amphibious things, mold and mustiness, boys' gym lockers—girls' gym lockers, too. Then we turned a corner and began to walk downhill, the smells getting stronger all the while. We took iron stairs down to another level; then we met a door.

We entered a large pool room.

"You girls aren't rich by any chance, are you?"

Addressing us in a French accent was a short, pudgy, kind-faced man, who stood near the edge of the pool in a stretchy blue bathing suit that looked completely dry. Waves of light reflected off the water onto him, the walls, the ceiling. Swimming around in the pool haphazardly were two young men. The Frenchman explained to us that the swimmers were his friends who came over when the ship was in port and their office was slow. "They are hoping to meet a millionaire," he laughed. "They always threaten not to leave the ship on time unless I produce one."

"Jean-Claude knows lots of millionaires," one of the swimmers said in an American accent. "But he won't share them with us. Will you, J.-C.?"

"It's my job to keep people like you away from them," Jean-Claude said good-naturedly, shrugging like a boy.

The other swimmer said something to the one who had spoken. I could not make out the words, but I could hear that he

was an American, too. They laughed. The one who had spoken
first swam over to the side, none too expertly. He draped his
thick elbows over the pool's rim. I could see he was heavy-
breasted and hairless. He reminded me of a boy in my class, big
and goofy and permanently embarrassed, whose blood ran clear
when he cut himself falling down in the schoolyard. The other
one, a much better swimmer, thin and dark, moved like a snake
in the water, making almost no splashes. Treading water invisi-
bly, he said to us: "Come on in."

"You come out," Mary Jane giggled.

I noticed that Mary Jane's posture had changed. One shoulder
was flung back; one dipped forward. She no longer slouched.
And I could guess that she was trying to catch the attention of
the dark one, who now was swimming over to the ladder at the
end of the pool where the diving board was. Mary Jane watched
as he reached the ladder, pulled himself up, then fell backwards
into the pool, making a blue explosion of water. He did the
backstroke over to the other side of the deep end, reversed
direction, swam until he was under the diving board, then made
a leap for it, and hung on with his long, brown arms. The
reflection of the water made his face look ghoulishly blue.

I looked around to see where Jean-Claude was; he was getting
dressed into a steward's uniform that was all laid out on a
wooden bench.

"Yes, come out," Jean-Claude said politely, stepping into his
pants. "It's time for everyone to come out now. The bell will
ring very soon."

The dark one ignored Jean-Claude, swimming over to Mary
Jane; the heavier one ignored him, too, and began to eye me. I
could add two and two just as well as anyone, and I saw I was
paired with him.

I took off my Ringo cap and ran my fingers through my un-
washed hair. Where was I getting my nerve? I was not one bit
frightened. The presence of Jean-Claude seemed to make it all
right, somehow. His cheeks glowed rosy and bright, and he, all
dressed now, from shoes to cap, looked especially fine. Almost
as authoritative as a policeman, but without the harshness of
the gun and the stick and the badge and the squawking radio.

Jean-Claude paced at the side of the pool. "You know what will happen! You know! You know!" Suddenly nervous now. "I will lose my job! You know this! If you don't leave here on time. And I wish you girls would leave, too. Go back to your staterooms."

"We don't have any staterooms," Mary Jane said haughtily.

Jean-Claude slapped his head.

The heavier one must have been the more considerate of the two, for he was swimming to the side; I'm sure he was preparing to haul himself out of the pool even as the other one swam into the center and Jean-Claude began shouting in French: *"Fiche le camp! Fiche le camp—!"* So the dark one swam back to the side, grabbed Jean-Claude by the leg, and pulled him in.

The water closed over Jean-Claude's head. And his hands fluttered like leaves on the surface, then sank beneath the surface, and the water was calm around him.

The heavier one and the dark one both scrambled, fighting over the ladder, to be the first one out of the pool. Mary Jane put a finger to her cheek. "Oh, dear," she said, like a heroine; she did not move. And neither did I. I watched the spot where Jean-Claude had disappeared, and waited for his head to bob up; silently I was rooting for him to recover with aplomb.

When Jean-Claude's head finally did appear again, his mouth was large and open and making a strange, inward gushing noise. His hands made a fluttering again, as if they were trying to lift him into the air. His elbows were working, too, but looked as if they were weighted down, like a marionette's elbows, pulled down by gravity.

I tried to read his face. He seemed unaware of everything but the water. There was no anger in his eyes, only wonder and terror at the water. Then his apple cheeks disappeared again, as if something were pulling him under, pulling him down by the legs.

The two young men were out of the pool now, watching, standing naked, having kicked off and away their bathing suits.

"What do you know? The bastard can't swim!" said the dark one.

They pulled on their clothes.

The men walked quickly, did not run, to the exit, their shoes in their hands, smoothing their heads like men running to a train, more important matters to attend to. They didn't look back, not even when Mary Jane called after them. Then she turned to me.

We both watched Jean-Claude pull himself along the edge of the pool to the ladder. His gaze was as sure and constant as steel. He was seeing something very clearly. I suddenly became frightened.

Mary Jane and I ran to the exit, ran out into the corridor. We fell into step with the gathering crowd, and moved along with them, men and women all together. A bell sounded over our heads. We kept close, arms touching, in step in the disorderly procession. We did not speak a word, but we kept close, as if huddled for protection.

# The Ring: Or,
# A Girl Confesses

"Though I am not naturally honest,
I am so sometimes by chance."
—Autolycus, *The Winter's Tale*

N OVEMBER, 1967. I am introduced to Renata at a drugstore near the high school. She is eating French fries and ketchup, and wearing a teal-blue wool jersey dress, gold necklace, and rabbit-fur coat. The dress is rich-looking and I wish it were mine. She acts as if she's between thirty and forty. She is seventeen. She keeps the rabbit-fur coat on—she must be cold or something.

I remember the clothes, even days later, because clothes, especially expensive ones, are an obsession of mine. I am fifteen, and modeling is my chief ambition, anorexia nervosa the mental disease of choice.

She is sitting in a booth in the drug store with a mutual friend—Chris Cranley—a very dour, bookish girl, with a tiny red mouth and squinty, black, unhappy eyes, who often blurts cruel things at me (and others) in the name of honesty. For example: "Angel, you really wouldn't be bad-looking if you didn't have those blackheads." But she is funny in her bald candor, and I like to hear the truth—sometimes. No illusions. It can be helpful to those bent on self-improvement. Besides, though I am obsessed by physical appearance, it is not my sole concern. Chris's verbal ability does attract me: her vocabulary would be too big to hide, even if she tried to.

When Renata speaks, I see buck teeth and braces and particles of food—and she has an acne-covered chin—so she isn't perfect; and the boy with her is puny and uninteresting, wearing a moronic hat and dazed rock-star expression—a known speed freak: drinking coffee, naturally. And yet Renata is the center of the group, and holding court without saying very much more than droll things about the French fries. Chris and I both watch her eat, especially when her vichyssoise arrives. I have never heard of a cold soup before. Even Chris is silent at this point, while Renata slurps.

We become friends, Renata and I. She seems to appreciate me. She comments favorably on my appearance, my clothes—a style all my own, she says. And I believe her. Such an old seventeen! She cannot be called beautiful, nor even pretty. She is thin, but has those awful teeth, and strange dyed hair like yellow feathers. Still, she does manage to be somehow attractive: she has a worldly grimness—like Chris's, but real. She looks not only old but wise, as if she can tell you things about yourself. Things you'd never guess.

"Those girls in their Ladybug outfits at the high school think they look so rich," she tells me. "But my friends in the city would laugh their heads off at such a presumption! They might wear a Ladybug outfit for fun, as a costume. Their clothes are made for them in Europe. Those girls in their Ladybug clothes don't know what real sums of money are. Angel, you look better in your imitation designer dresses bought off the rack at Alexander's— from a distance, anyway."

She lies back on her bed, with her shoes on, smoking lazily. I am trying on her clothes, taken from a closet so full the rack is bent with the weight. She even has two dresses exactly alike: because she forgot she bought it once, she bought it again.

The house where Renata lives with her father and stepmother

is so immense not only a child, but even I, could get lost in it. The driveway is blue gravel and winds around. The front door opens into a hallway of black-and-white tile that always puts me in mind of a game with live players. Above, a monstrous chandelier. Off to the left, a dark-wood paneled study with guns in cases on the wall—antiques. A large, brilliantly white kitchen is down a few steps to the right, bowls on the counters, toppling with fresh fruit ripened just to perfection. And there, with her hand on the refrigerator door is . . . Sondra—Renata's father's third wife—about to open it exactly as she opens the prize refrigerator door on *Treasure Hunt,* the afternoon TV game show. She still has her TV makeup on, a cheerfulness painted onto her face, and fear, not hate, in her round, warm eyes. She fears Renata just as much as she fears her own husband of these few, short months. I can tell by the way she talks about him. I fear him, too, and I haven't even met him. All that we see in this house is his doing.

Chris Cranley is angry with me, because I have stolen Renata. But I don't care. Chris is such a hateful person. A mean, little being. And we are friends no longer. It happens this way: I borrow her jeans, and do not return them. I wear them to the park, to the beach, to Renata's house. One day, Chris comes over, storms into my house, up the stairs, snatches the jeans off the floor, and drives away. She is probably disappointed that she found the jeans so quickly—she didn't get to throw things out of my drawers and closet, digging like a little terrier. She is probably angry that she didn't get the chance to tear them off me.

Renata lends me clothes, lots of them, even the rabbit-fur coat. Also, a navy-blue wool coat and a pearl on a gold chain. To say nothing of blouses, skirts, and shoes. I am not exactly her size. I am closer to Chris's, though thinner than Chris, but not as thin as Renata—but Renata says I look all right. And dressed up, we go places: to the Benjamins', for example.

The Benjamins have a house like an old castle, but there is also a new part with a room on stilts and a man-hole cover in the middle of the floor. Lift the cover, and fish through it if you like. No one ever does. It's just for show, I'm told. What exactly is the purpose of the Volkswagen in the pool outside, a little Benjamin boy asks, but never discovers. He keeps after his mother about it; she is one of the Benjamins' older daughters. (The youngest one is Renata's friend.) Of the car in the pool the young mother says, "They are trying to see if it's going to float, just for fun. They want to know if it's airtight, like it's supposed to be. Isn't that right, Philip?" she asks her husband, who ignores her—he is talking to another man, both of them with drinks of gold liquid in their hands.

"Is there somebody in the car?" the boy asks.

"No, honey."

It is Christmas time here. We are looking at the lighted pool through the large-paned windows. Then Mrs. Benjamin, with a honey-colored bun at the nape of her neck and idle hands that never fidget, calls us all to sit down at the dining-room table. She presses a button on the floor with her foot, and a little Hispanic maid scurries in.

I say very little at this family gathering. When we get home to Renata's, though, she tells me that Mrs. Benjamin said I have "what is called 'an old soul'—she said you know deep down in your gut what it takes most of the rest of us all our lives to learn." I go to sleep happy, believing this to be true, because someone like Mrs. Benjamin has said it. And Renata seems to believe it, too.

I awaken to the sounds of Renata shouting in the kitchen far below. Sleepily I follow the corridors to the sounds, and find Renata and Sondra. Renata is startled by my presence; she storms past me up the stairs. There is nothing for me to do but follow, but Sondra calls me back. "Angel, would you like some breakfast?" I would. And we sit and talk. She is sweet; my shoulders relax. We gossip. We talk about something neutral. Not about Renata, but Chris. "You know, I believe she's had relations," Sondra says in her soft, Midwestern way. "She just seems so hard." I nod in wonderment, not agreement—I just don't know enough about such things; but later it will turn out that Chris has been lured onto the couch of the admissions officer of a college which doesn't even accept her. She's not so smart.

February, 1968, three months later. A Friday night. "Money! Money!" Renata is shouting from the open window of her cab. An infernal orange light blinks on as she struggles with the door.

I go out to meet her with a wad of bills in my hand. I wear no shoes—I've taken them off, sitting waiting for her in front of the TV—so my shoulders wince with each step I take across the cold sidewalk.

"This reminds me exactly of the night I ran away from my *mother*!" Renata says as she and I struggle to the porch with her heavy luggage. She laughs through her crooked teeth, but I can see her glittering eyes; in the frantic phone call she made to me, too, I could tell she had been crying. "I even had on this same Givenchy scarf. But I didn't bring any *clothes* that time. I tried wearing Sondra's stuff, but of course everything was way too big. She was a lot thinner then, when my father first met her. And maybe I could have fit into those clothes she used to wear. But the minute they got married, she threw out anything old and started buying all new. And *spreading*! You've seen her hips!" She sighs. "But at least I had them to run away to that time. Funny, I'm running away *from* them this time. And this time, all I have is you!"

As Renata speaks, I usher her into the house—a two-family, three stories: we have the two top floors. I know from the look on my mother's face that she has been watching us out the window and must have seen me pay the cab driver.

"Who's got who?" my mother asks, peering at Renata through her cat glasses so hopelessly out of date. She is large and flabby; she just shows too much—not only flesh, but the way she feels.

"*Che fanno?*" my grandmother asks my mother, like a shadow, wearing a too-short black dress—her knees show, rough from cleaning and prayer. Her red hands, loosely braided, rest on the pillow of her stomach.

"Who's got who?" my mother repeats. "I heard you say something like that."

"Renata is angry with her stepmother—" I begin.

"Angel told me she's on TV," says my mother. "A model—that's nice work, I bet."

"*She* calls it 'acting!'" says Renata. "Do you believe it?"

"I haven't seen the show. I'm at work when it's on, but my mother watches—"

"Eh?" My grandmother leans forward to have my mother

explain. When she understands, she nods, unimpressed.

"People say I could be a better model than she is," says Renata, removing her coat. "If I didn't have these decorations." She points with a dirty broken fingernail to the acne on her chin.

"Renata, do you want something to eat?" my mother asks the spindly girl. "I've got some delicious *biscotti*—you ever have those? You dip them in a little red wine—"

"Thank you, no, Mrs. Scalfani, although I know you're a chef—"

"A what?" My mother looks at me. She, who is a cook at an elementary school cafeteria.

"—I think I'll just go straight to bed," says Renata.

My mother throws another glance my way.

"Renata is staying over, is that all right, Mom?" I am addressing the carpet.

"I saw the suitcases," says my mother, a hand on her mismatched plaid hips.

"I'm never going back there!" Renata announces, then starts looking around. "Are the bedrooms—?"

"Upstairs," I say quickly. My father is snoring in the bedroom off the living room.

"I've just got to get some sleep," Renata says. "I'm so depressed, and sleep's the only cure for it, I've found. Sondra's that bouncy type who never gets depressed. Or claims not to, anyway. I've been depressed for four or five years now."

"Have a little warm milk with money, I mean, honey in it," offers my mother, but her eyes behind her glasses are narrowed. "If you don't want the wine."

"Thanks, but I took a Seconal on the cab ride over. Without water." Renata smiles. My mother's unplucked eyebrows go up. "I'm getting to be pretty good at that," Renata adds. "G'night." She floats up the stairs on her way to the third floor, where my grandmother and I sleep. I start to follow her, to avoid any more questions from my mother and perhaps to answer Renata's, but my mother calls me back and whispers loudly, "What is going on?"

"She's staying over, isn't that okay? I've slept over at her house enough times."

"What was she crying about?"

"I don't know. She's tired. She can sleep with me in my bed. Or I'll sleep on the floor—I don't care."

"What's the trouble at home?"

"She hates her stepmother, that's all."

"That's all?"

"And her father, too, I guess."

"Oh, that's all." My mother slaps her side, and gives a little laugh.

Above us, Renata can be heard swearing as she tries to turn on a broken light switch at the top of the stairs.

"I'll be right there," I call out.

"No rush," Renata returns. "I should learn my way around. If I'm going to be staying here for any length of time."

My mother gives me a piercing look. I escape up the stairs.

The next morning, when I come downstairs, I find my father sitting at the kitchen table, eating his breakfast. My father is overweight, with a soft round belly underneath his white T-shirt. He usually sits around the house in his T-shirt and a pair of khaki work pants. This morning he wears a black cardigan sweater over his shoulders. I recognize it as one of my grandmother's— she must have put it on him, and this time he didn't resist. He isn't feeling well, and hasn't been for a while. I sit down beside him. "Hi, Dad."

"Hey, baby." He pats my arm.

"Renata still sleeping?" my mother asks me, standing at the stove. She's wearing one of my father's old pairs of pants. My grandmother sits at the window, looking down into her garden plot in the frozen back yard, but turns to me to learn the answer to the question I've been posed.

I nod, and won't look at either of the two women, but neither will my father look at me. He is carefully mopping up a broken egg yolk with a rough crust of bread.

I get up and go to the stove to pour myself a cup of coffee, and see that my mother is cooking large quantities of fried potatoes and bacon as well as eggs and toast. A company break-fast. On Renata's behalf. I groan to myself, and perhaps a little out loud. I hate all the cooking that goes on in this house. I am always awakened by the smell of cooking on these weekend mornings. It follows me everywhere, too, by way of my clothes. I resent the food. Still, I am ravenous; I have to eat, and the longer I wait to eat, the more hungrily I do so, and the more pleased my mother and grandmother look.

"She doesn't really think she's going to stay here past this weekend, does she?" asks my mother.

I shrug, stirring my coffee.

"What am I supposed to say when her father calls me?"

"He won't call."

"He knows where she is, doesn't he?"

"He might, but he won't call."

"Her stepmother—Sondra—will call then."

"Maybe, but you don't have to say anything to her, either, if you don't want to."

"What do you mean, I don't have to say anything to her?"

"She doesn't have any power over Renata."

"The hell she doesn't."

My mother takes a piece of bacon from the pan and starts chewing thoughtfully. My grandmother has asked her for a translation of what is being said, and my mother is giving herself time to switch from English to Italian.

"I mean," I add in this interval, "Sondra's only twenty-nine."

"And as I told Sondra herself, he never keeps them past thirty," says Renata.

She is standing in the doorway of the kitchen, wearing her apricot silk bathrobe and carrying a tiny coffee pot. She scuffs in her fuzzy slippers, once pink, now gray, over to the sink. I am struck by how wrong her previously wonderful bed clothes look in this house.

"I've got some coffee right here, Renata," my mother says, pointing to the percolator.

"What kind?" Renata asks.

"What?"

"What type of coffee?"

"I don't know. A&P?"

Renata makes a quick gesture to signify no, and pats her

bathrobe pocket. "I've got some French Roast right here."

My grandmother says something to my mother about what she is seeing down in the garden. Even in winter, when there is nothing growing, she watches for things down there.

"What did she say?" Renata asks me.

"*I* don't know."

"She said," my mother tells her, "that the Mangialardo's cat's doing his business down there. In summer, she'd shake the broom at him, but in winter she likes to see him digging: good for fertilizer."

This makes my mother and grandmother laugh, and I laugh, too, in spite of myself. My father smiles only a little, and keeps eating his meal. Renata sports an expression of disgust, and thinking perhaps that she has found a comrade in the silent, ill man, she brings herself to him at the table.

"Hello," she says, offering him her hand, straight-armed.

He looks up at her in surprise, as if he had not expected her ever to acknowledge him; he takes her slim, white hand.

"Looks like snow," he says, glancing toward the window.

"Won't that be grand?" says Renata, speaking in a tone I've never heard her use before.

"Oh, I don't know. Did Angel tell you I drive the snowplow?"

"She told me you drive trucks. You must be very strong. And the snowplow, too? But is there only one plow for the whole town, and you drive it?"

"No! There's sixteen—, no—." He looks up at the ceiling like a schoolboy. "No, twenty-two snowplows we got now."

"That's wonderful!" says Renata, clasping her hands against her robe.

"I don't know about how wonderful it is," says my father, "but we keep things moving all right."

As they have been speaking, he has been arranging his cleaned plate, the dirty utensils on either side of it, folded his soiled napkin. Now he nods at Renata cordially, pushes back his chair, and leaves the table.

My mother and grandmother make comments about him in Italian, gesturing to his empty place and the doorway he has just walked through. I catch some fear in my mother's voice, but soon enough she is cutting off her own mother, and turns abruptly to Renata, obviously to change a painful subject: "So what's this fight with your stepmother about?"

"She's a thief," Renata says plainly. She is back at the stove, administering to her little coffee pot, my mother with her two frying pans going, but keeping out of Renata's way.

"Oh, yeah? Wha'd she steal?" asks my mother with real interest, and I am listening intently, too.

"Oh, only an heirloom diamond ring appraised at three thousand dollars."

"And whose diamond ring was this?"

"Mine."

"What's a young girl like you doing with a diamond ring like that?"

"My grandmother left it to me when she died. Can you imagine someone stealing an heirloom from her own stepdaughter? It's like a fairy tale. The wicked stepmother steals the diamond ring and puts a deadly curse on the stepdaughter."

"You believe that?"

"I might. Will you excuse me, please?" Renata says. "I'm not really feeling well."

"That's because you need a nice big breakfast, and then a nice walk downtown. You girls both need some fresh air. Why don't you do that? Angel has to go downtown to get me some chopped meat, anyway."

"I do?"

"Yes, you do."

"Angel, you go without me," says Renata. "I'm really feeling like hell."

"Sure."

"Good. I'm going back to bed." Renata takes her coffee pot off the stove, a cup from the open cupboard, and leaves the kitchen.

"I can't believe nobody's going to call to find out her whereabouts last night," says my mother.

"That's how they are," I insist, believing it only about her father, not Sondra. I know that Sondra's not a thief. "Why do you think she doesn't want to live with them anymore?"

"But she can't stay here."

"She told me she'd pay you," I say, without enthusiasm.

"I don't want her money!"

"Well, she's going to give you some anyway."

"I won't take it."

"Suit yourself."

I go up to my bedroom, and find Renata presumably asleep, her face to the wall. I get dressed, and walk and pose as if she were watching me, giving me pointers; as if I were in the presence of many other rich girls as well, who accept me totally, even look up to me. This is my habit, but today I feel foolish going through this favorite ritual.

I have put on my shopping outfit, which consists of a long skirt, blazer, plus a crazy hat which I found at a secondhand store on a school trip into the city. Renata and I told our teacher that Renata was ill and that we were going to take a cab to her father's office, where she could lie down. We would take the train home with him, we said. Of course we just went shopping.

My hat looks wrong. Perhaps I've worn it too many times. I need something new. I vow that I will not go to the huge discount warehouse with my mother to pick up something on sale. The smell of that place is horrible—of popcorn and fried foods bubbling—it gets on the clothes and, even when you bring them home, can not be gotten rid of.

I wish I could go again to the shops that I visited with Renata in the city. It seems that no one buys items in those places without asking loads of questions. It seems to be a part of what you pay for—the attention, the chance to make the salesman get sweaty, run back and forth all over the shop, climb up on a high ladder, before he can finally relax behind the counter, ringing up the sale, his fingers looking happy as his face. I wish I could make a salesclerk feel and look as happy as Renata made the salesclerks look all over the city that day.

I use a fountain pen of Renata's filled with green ink to write her a note, saying when I'll be back. Renata has so many other colors of ink—brown, violet, peacock blue—it intrigues me that these colors of ink even exist, since blue is perfectly adequate for anything anyone will ever write. Any color but blue is superfluous—even blue-black and black. These other colors are for pleasure, for fun, for whim. And the fact that they exist for others makes me want to become one of these others, long before I'm old.

Just before I leave for downtown I check again for the small, hard thing in my pocket.

Monday morning, and my mother and I are talking in the kitchen. My grandmother is the tiny black shadow by her side once again.

"She's going to be late for school—where is she?" my mother shouts.

"She's sick; she's not going to school."

"Daddy's not going to work," my mother says, with a fallen face.

I act surprised, but I have already noticed that the door of my parents' bedroom is closed.

Then I notice that my grandmother has been crying in the way she does, without the wetness of tears.

"Carla," my father calls to my mother from the bedroom. We three women stand there in silence for a moment, under the buzzing kitchen lights.

My mother goes in to see him. They argue a moment; then she comes back out. "Your father is going to work after all."

My grandmother sits down at her post, looking down into the frozen garden.

"I thought he was sick," I say.

"He is, but he doesn't think it's right for him to be alone in the house all day with Renata."

"Where's Gramma going to be?"

"This is the day she goes up to the church for a couple of hours."

"So? That's just a couple of hours."

"He says he couldn't relax with Renata around here, anyway."

"But that's ridiculous! He's got to—"

"Don't say your father is ridiculous!" My mother gives me a slap. "I gotta get that girl outa my house!" she shouts. I follow her up the stairs. "You!" She pulls the groggy-faced, flailing Renata out of the bed.

Recklessly, she drives us both to the high school, with Renata's luggage. I have the ring in my pocket, having put it there early this morning, having expected to wear it at school, since I thought Renata wouldn't be there.

Renata says: "That woman slapped you, didn't she?"

I feel sorry for her.

August, 1960. I am eight years old, and not particularly hungry, but I am in the Food Center with my mother, standing by a bushelbasket of peanuts, and reach in. I do not check first to see if someone is watching me. This basket is for dipping into, isn't it? It is uncovered, the peanuts look so tempting, and what is more, the basket is exactly at my level. I don't have to stoop or reach.

How many do I take? Three or four. But just as I am putting them into my pocket, I catch sight of . . . him!—the produce man, shaking a finger at me, his face looking stern, disappointed as any father's. He shakes his curly head slowly, but his eyes don't move. They keep boring into me. Luckily, my mother has pushed her cart on already—she is out of sight. But still I face a terrible choice. To put the peanuts back is to admit that I have taken them at all. To keep them is to risk his coming over to me, to shout, to lay a hand on my shoulder. Perhaps to hit me.

I decide to run. Out of the store. I run to the car. I have never left a store before, to wait out in the car. My mother will wonder where I am, but I won't go back into that store. I won't, for many years it turns out. I will always wait in the car thereafter. It will be my absolutely first and last episode of shoplifting. I will never steal from a store again.

Eating the peanuts is, of course, completely out of the question.

September, 1970, and I am ill. In more ways than one. I am ill many days, lying in his bed. When he goes out, I take the quarters from his bureau, get dressed, drag myself to the corner grocery store, and buy some cottage cheese. Back at his apartment, I pour honey into the carton, stir it up, and eat, eat it all.

Then I wash the spoon, and put the carton into the incinerator down the hall. I feel much better. And sleep until I am well.

When he comes home, he is pleased to see that I have eaten nothing still, as far as he can see—he likes his women thin—but later he asks me if I have taken by any chance the silver dollars his grandfather gave him. Silver dollars? That must mean I was gypped by the grocery-store clerk, who only gave me pennies in change.

I deny everything.

June, 1975. I confess the crime about the diamond ring to a certain new friend, and the way I do it is like the giving of a gift, the gift of candor, self revelation, even though at the time I do not know exactly what it is that I am revealing.

I describe the way I wore the ring to Renata's house, by accident, the following cold November—a little over a year after I had met her in the drug store. Chris Cranley and Renata both had gone away to college—I still had one more year left of high school—and it was Renata's idea for us three to meet for a chat on Thanksgiving weekend at her house.

I know just what I was wearing—a demure gray mid-calf-length wool dress (from a secondhand shop in town), gray stockings, gray shoes—and the ring! It had become such a habit to wear it, and I had tried to remember to take it off, but must have forgotten. Then, again, some say there is no such thing as an accident.

I had just arrived; I was gesticulating, describing the drive over, the rains of late November. Wet leaves. Treacherous— the car had spun—

"That ring!" Renata shrieked. "Where did you get that ring?"

"Oh, this?" I looked at it, took it off with nonchalance, as if I found it annoying, and handed it to her. "It's yours. Remember you lent it to me?"

"This ring? I would never lend this ring." She jammed it on her finger, and looked at me in profound puzzlement, but she said nothing more.

"Well, now you've got it back; that's the important thing," soothed Sondra. Then I saw Renata and Sondra, and even Chris,

move closer to each other at the table, where they were drinking tea.

No one mentioned the ring further that evening, though I
frequently caught one or the other of them staring at me: someone who would apparently steal from a friend and show no
remorse. I felt more composed than usual.

I never saw any one of them again.

# Before Sewing
# One Must Cut

I T WAS 1968, and I hadn't been paying a bit of attention.
I was fifteen years old.

Then suddenly Mr. Perrotti, the chief groundskeeper for the
church, who lived on church property with his family—whose
two daughters actually *swam* with the nuns, regularly saw nuns
in *bathing suits*, in bathing *caps* (with chin straps, they reported),
and, God knows, so might have he—walked out.

It was a Saturday afternoon lecture in the high-school gymnasium, and he did not leave quietly.

Father Daniel DeCicco was speaking about the Vietnam War
in his youthful singsong that made me realize he was really just
an altar boy who had grown up. The gym was filled with Sister
Corita banners, someone's private collection of colors, lent to
the school for the occasion, flying high above our heads. My
eye had been caught by them. I wasn't listening to the small,
dark, lean Father DeCicco any more closely than I listened to
him in church—that is, for the voice rather than the actual words,
except when he threw in some Beatles or Monkees lyrics ("I'm
a Believer..."), which he did none too adroitly: it always
sounded so adultishly forced. Then, the next thing I knew, Mr.
Perrotti was out in the aisle yelling and shaking his fist at him.

Mr. Perrotti was related, though only by marriage, to a famous football player, but he himself was big. He looked as if he were wearing shoulder pads underneath his clothing, though his pants drooped in the seat. He was the bus driver I'd had from kindergarten through the eighth grade. He, in addition to the groundswork, general maintenance, caretaking, gravedigging, etc., drove us children to school; drove the old nuns to the dentist in their gray station wagon (when a younger nun wasn't free to do it); drove the priests' gray Cadillac to the shop for a tune-up.

He also seemed to me to be my second father (even before my first one passed away). It had nothing to do with my mother. It had only to do with me. As a child, I had admired him. He seemed always to make it a point to tell the truth, or at least to tell whatever he was thinking. He had been in the Service with my real father and had shown me a snapshot of my father and himself at the Air Force barracks, bath towels wrapped around their middles, nothing else, both of them eating dripping ice-cream cones in the North Carolina heat.

He'd shown me this to tell me something about my father, something a father wouldn't necessarily have told his daughter, himself. This was when my father was ill and looking about a hundred years old.

Mr. Perrotti, whose first name was Lester (anglicized from Leonardo), had taken a special liking to me when I was a play-mate of his daughters. Of all their friends I knew he liked me the best. I could tell that he liked the way I acted. He definitely liked the way I got his jokes. He probably felt sorry for me, too, now that my father was dead. I also knew he expected no less of me. He would say to his girls, one a year younger than I, one a year older: "Hey, why can't you two do like 'Maria'?" He still called me "Maria," even though Juliet Leeuwen had been given the lead in our eighth-grade production of *The Sound of Music*. Two years later he was still trying to tell me I should have had it. (I'd stopped reminding him that I'd been too shy even to audition.) This was mostly when I saw him at the church or somewhere else uptown, not at his house, because I didn't go over there to hang around with his daughters much anymore. We were starting to have different friends. Overweight ("good eaters"), in the "B" track, and one of them with a bad case of psoriasis, Paula and Joanie Perrotti now tried to make up for their shortcomings with loudness, and I'd grown embarrassed for them.

Mr. Perrotti was wearing a suit on the day of his outburst. Strange sight, him in a suit? Not so strange: he wore one every Sunday to the ten o'clock Mass. The anger wasn't unfamiliar to him, either, but his target was a new one. The young Father DeCicco stopped talking and lowered his prematurely bald head.

Sonny Perrotti, the chief lifeguard at the beach for three summers running, stood in the aisle with his father, looking solemn and proud, hands behind his back. He was the Perrottis' beloved only son. Every summer in his orange bathing suit he boxed boys' ears and made them eat their beach cards. Girls liked him, but not dozens of them—only one at a time. On his breaks, he did not show off for a crowd with the rescue surfboard; he merely mooned (or argued) in the shade of the pavilion with his latest. Then, back up into the chair to blow his whistle every five minutes.

Sonny did not look at all surprised by his father's rage. He wore the same self-satisfied expression as the ushers in church who stood along the side walls during Mass, waiting to rush up the aisles with their long-handled collection baskets and sweep them under everybody's nose.

Mr. Perrotti kept shouting, walking backwards and forwards down the center aisle made by rows of metal folding chairs. He looked like a very large bird, upset. That is, he looked as if at any moment he'd sprout wings and fly around the place. Or else slap someone right across the face. He had a strange, mottled skin, like camouflage, on his own face. He claimed it was a tropical skin problem he'd picked up during his years in the Service. I had no reason to believe that he was lying, though I remember once my father had belittled that line. It was also my father who had told me Mr. Perrotti had never quite got over the fact that he hadn't seen action.

"Action," "Missing in Action," "POW's," "this country," Mr. Perrotti was saying now. I had an aisle seat and looked up at him, into one of his armpits, as he flailed his arms, and I caught a scent of after-shave lotion. Sitting on the aisle in class, when a nun walked by, you could look up and see underneath her cardboard bib: her neck, the outline of her breasts covered by minutely layered folds of coarse black cloth (nuns were braless, it was plain), and catch a smell of her, of nuns, of harsh soap, of scrubbing, of trying to be scentless and failing. There were both opened and unopened bottles of after-shave in our medicine cabinet at home. Would my mother eventually throw them into the trash can, or would I?

"Anytime, day or night," Mr. Perrotti said. He had a pointy chin and seemed to be pointing with it as well as with his finger at Father DeCicco. "Right now, go over there," "me and my only son," "we're ready," "our country, God bless it!" Sonny stood tall, legs apart, hands still locked behind him.

When the old Father Brumley, our pastor, tried to calm Mr. Perrotti, with his wrinkled, reasoning hands, he only managed to fan Mr. Perrotti's ire all the more. Now he was talking about "faggots," "free lovers," "Greenwich Village," and "mixed marriage."

Father DeCicco listened with his head bowed. Or else he might have been praying.

He was a handsome priest. We girls, including Mr. Perrotti's own two daughters, called him, gigglingly, "cute." Actually, he looked exactly like an Italian-American movie actor, but with less hair—one of the young, tragic-eyed ones, like Al Pacino in *The Godfather, Part I*, only we wouldn't know that for another few years.

At my father's funeral (it had been earlier that same fall), I was offered a job after school and on weekends by one of the other priests in the parish, the fastidious Father Gerard. When he asked me, I was standing at the muddy gravesite, a red carnation in my hand. Caroline Castiglione's father, the undertaker, had handed it to me, wearing a rubbery smile, surprisingly sincere. I had on an old black skirt and runs in both stockings from having caught them on fallen twigs I'd stepped over on the cemetery path. As we spoke, others were talking, too, and I had to ask him to repeat what he had said to me. For one, my Aunt Janey was complaining loudly about how the cemetery was kept up. And why shouldn't artificial flowers be allowed? Why not? She wanted to know. She wanted an answer from somebody and she wanted it now.

The Knights of Columbus paid the bulk of our funeral bills. Money was a problem. My mother also needed time alone; with a job I'd be out of her way. So, one day shortly after Mr. Perrotti's demonstration, I finally took Father Gerard up on his offer, and walked up the stone steps of the rectory to pay him a visit.

The church, the rectory (where the priests lived), and the elementary school I had attended were all on a choice piece of property in town, on the main avenue. The high school, the convent, and the Perrottis' house were all out in the back country, on a former estate complete with the pool where the nuns swam, stables (empty), and a rose garden with sculpture, where the Perrotti daughters and I had liked to play hide-and-seek when we were younger. The Bishop of Bridgeport, an egg-shaped man, had consecrated it all, including the Perrottis' house, garage, truck, and two cars—one of them a Mustang convertible that Sonny sometimes drove.

The kitchen of the rectory was a clean, orderly place of no raised voices, just like the rest of the house. The back door opened out onto a walled, well-tended garden of green and gold and flickering black shadows. I could see only a corner of it from where I stood in the doorway leading into the kitchen from the long front hallway.

Father Gerard stood beside me, knotting and unknotting his arms. He made me think of pure intelligence, a bolt of it, like the angels, only much less calm. The hair of the slim, perpetually nervous priest was white, ethereally, though he probably was no older than my father would have been. His legs were long and thin and seemed to be always in motion, bending like straps, and the black priest-pants he wore were surprisingly tight. I stood self-consciously in my blue-gray school uniform, and he did the talking for both of us.

"There's a way to a successful interview, for a job, or for school, or for anything, don't you think? When you go to your college interviews, the admissions officer will ask you, 'Well, are you a good student or a bad student?' And if you say, 'I'm a good student, Father!' won't *you* sound conceited. By the same token, I *don't* believe you'll be wanting to say, 'Oh, I'm a bad student!' So what do you do?"

A Hispanic woman was down on her knees, scrubbing the kitchen floor with a brush. Father Gerard introduced me to her: "Maria Cristina," rolling his r's and moving his hands as if he were conducting a choir.

Maria Cristina stood—a small, erect young woman, very calm. Her face was smooth and brown, her smile simple and relaxed. She dried her hands on her apron, looking as contented as a businessman's wife. Immediately I envied her.

Rocking back and forth on his heels, Father Gerard remarked that Maria Cristina had worked for them six years. Smiling and coloring with embarrassment, the little woman rubbed the counter with a cloth, looking almost saintly, actually dignified in her menial work. I thought: she must be beyond any sinful passions of her own. I also thought: I should take my cues from her.

Father Gerard must have been asking me for a second time if I wanted some tea, and finally I heard him and said yes.

He spoke to Maria Cristina in a histrionic Spanish, and they laughed together about his inability to put a tea tray together. I looked at his long white fingers, the fingers of a pampered man. At last she got things down from the cupboards for him, using a step-stool to get the extra sugar from the cannister to refill the bowl.

I saw that Maria Cristina was wearing little pink Capezio flats, the kind that everybody, including myself, was wearing lately— when I wasn't in my school uniform, that is. They made her feet look attractive and feminine. Her fingernails were painted, too, I noticed as I watched her put two fragile-looking cups and saucers on a tray.

Everything is going to be all right, I thought.

I was given the job of answering the door and the phone after Father Brumley's secretaries had gone home—that is, on weekdays from five to nine—and also on both weekend days, from one to nine. The main reason for my being there was in case the hospital called to ask for a priest to give a patient the Sacrament of Extreme Unction. There was always a priest in the house, on call, and I was to buzz that priest's bedroom on the telephone intercom and tell him what room in the hospital to go to.

This sounds exciting, maybe, but most of the hours I spent there were extremely boring, endlessly long, and fraught with temptations, despite my pile of homework. People seemed hardly ever to die, or if they did, they did not call for a priest.

On Saturdays, the priest on call also would tell me his confessional number so I could run and get him out of there, if necessary. That only happened once, and it was Father DeCicco on whose cubicle door I had to knock. For a small man he moved quickly, taking long, powerful strides. His black cassock swept the dusty sidewalks between the church and the rectory's front door. I had to run to keep up with him.

He unzipped his cassock right there in the rectory's front hallway and stepped out of it before running with it over his arm upstairs to his room. "Thanks, hon'," he threw back over his shoulder.

Underneath the cassock he was wearing the regulation black priest-pants and a white V-necked undershirt, and he had scuffed black loafers on his feet.

He sped away in his electric-blue Volkswagen Beetle.

I sat at a desk in a bay window in a room at the front of the rectory. It was filled with exotic knickknacks that Father Gerard, Father Brumley, and others had brought back from their travels all over the world. Out the window was my world—by that I mean Main Street.

Sometimes people came to the rectory door, looking for a handout. I was to keep them waiting outside on the doorstep and buzz the priest on call. He would give the person the prescribed amount of money in a manila envelope. People, women mostly, sometimes came with suitcases, requesting Father De-Cicco. I tried so hard to hear what they were saying (and, alternately, tried to ignore the temptation to listen). They would sit together in one of the parlors off the main hallway with the door closed. Afterwards, Father DeCicco would walk the woman to her car, his arm around her waist. I watched the arm of Father DeCicco encircling the waist of Teresa Masters for fifteen minutes one day. She leaned into his shoulder, crying. Her husband was the policeman who crossed people at the corner by the bank with the clock.

On the wall directly across from my desk there was a modern painting of Christ on the cross: an aerial view; the painter's eye had been only about three feet above the crown of thorns. I liked this painting a lot, not only because it was as soothingly familiar as my bedroom wallpaper by now, but also because I knew it meant something I did not quite understand—that particular angle of vision meant something special, I mean. And I caught myself wondering if even the priests knew exactly what it meant. One day I was idly studying the painting once again, when Father Gerard flew into the room, saying with his arm thrust out towards me: "Now, *that's* 'demure.'"

He had Sonny Perrotti in tow. Sonny, who'd shaved his head for a swim meet with Precious Blood, who'd shaved *all* his body hair—*everywhere*, according to his sisters—was being prepped for the College Boards by Father Gerard on weekends, as a special favor to the whole Perrotti family.

Sonny rubbed his nose with both hands, abruptly, like a fly. He looked particularly insect-like without any hair.

"'Demure!'" Father Gerard intoned. "'Sedate in manner or behavior; reserved; feigning modesty or shyness. See synonyms at *shy*.'" Then he turned on his heel, and Sonny followed, still scratching himself, and giving the impression that he was being led by the ear, although Father Gerard had not touched him.

Later that same day, after Sonny had gone home, I could hear Father DeCicco and the old Father Brumley in the dining room, chatting over a late Saturday lunch. They exchanged witty stories, using many voices, and asked each other demonstratively for seconds on the food that Maria Cristina had so lovingly prepared.

I liked these two priests, liked them far better than Father Gerard even though he was the one who had hired me. I couldn't ever imagine telling my troubles to him. I might have told them to Father Brumley, but would he understand? He might even fall asleep. It could be only Father DeCicco, if that time ever came.

Father DeCicco not only had many who sought his counselling; he had many personal friends, too. He got by far the most phone calls of anyone, often long-distance. There was no time he considered the phone an intrusion. He never said, "Hold my calls for the rest of the afternoon," the way Father Gerard did, pressing on his temples. Unlike Father Gerard in another instance, he never made sure that I had hung up my extension before he started speaking.

I had the feeling that Father DeCicco and Father Gerard did not like each other. I had the feeling that Father Gerard had taken Mr. Perrotti's side on the afternoon of the anti-war lecture. Father Gerard hated Communists. Once, he told me a long story of how one single Communist Party member at an American high school had convinced nearly his entire class to join his subversive efforts. (I couldn't help being impressed by such a persuasive young person.) Perhaps Father Gerard actually hated Father DeCicco. I thought: I will have to protect him.

While Fathers DeCicco and Brumley lunched, Father Gerard, who'd retired upstairs, suddenly ran downstairs and flung himself around in the hallway. He was crying and bearing news that he'd heard on his radio:

"An electric fan! An electrocution!" He put his face in his hands.

"He said it would kill him if he ever had to leave the monastery and so it has," Father Brumley said in quiet wonder.

"Did he really say that?" Father DeCicco asked in his boyish voice.

"He did." Father Brumley coughed respectfully.

December, 1968, and Thomas Merton was dead, only it would be over a decade before I would truly learn who he was, reading about his dissolution, conversion, subsequent faith, subsequent doubts in books from a secondhand bookstore.

Because I spent so much time at the rectory, next door to the church, I stopped going to Mass, as if the long hours and close proximity made up for my absence. Because all the priests heard my voice on the telephone intercom, disembodied, and (I felt sure) could recognize it as me sight unseen, I stopped going to confession. I planned to have a lengthy one somewhere else—in Rowayton or Milford—someday. As soon as I learned to drive and got my license I would go. (I walked to the rectory; it wasn't very far from my house.)

Maria Cristina lived close by, too, and though we never saw each other except at the rectory, we became friends. We devised a little language we both could understand, and she fed me things. When I learned that Maria Cristina had three children at home, her being at the rectory made less sense to me. Who was taking care of them? They took care of each other, she told me.

Maria Cristina and I sat around the kitchen table and smoked. Supplying myself with cigarettes was an endless problem, due to the expense. I gave my mother the money I made here, and I certainly couldn't bring myself to bum endlessly from the hard-working Maria Cristina.

I took to sneaking upstairs and searching the rooms of the priests who smoked. (Father Gerard actually was the only one: I used the forays as an excuse to snoop in the non-smokers' rooms as well.) I knew who was home and who wasn't: they all told me, so I'd know whether to buzz their rooms or just take messages. Sometimes, especially on Saturday nights after Maria Cristina had gone home, I was the only one in the whole place. Even the priest on call would be out, though he would have given me the number where he might be reached.

I crept up the red-carpeted stairway one Saturday evening. And be assured, there was no reason for me to be up on the second floor of this place: the ladies' room which Maria Cristina and I used was off the kitchen. If caught, I had no excuse whatsoever. None except that I might have heard voices (preferably celestial) or smelled smoke, I suppose. Even so, I regularly took my chances, as on this night, when, with pounding heart, I pushed open the unlatched door of Father DeCicco's room.

I found, quite simply, the usual mess: pajamas on the unmade bed, underwear in a circle on the Oriental rug, packets of Carnation Slender (later, I would learn he was so thin because he fasted for peace on liquids-only for three out of the five weekdays), and other signs of life. The unusual item was on his desk:

a bonus—an unfinished letter written in his own scribbly hand. Did I try to resist reading it? I wish I had; the words shocked me:

> *I pray you will trust your instincts and lean into this. That you will permit it to cut you, heal you, and cut you again. That you will stare at it into its own center. And that you will accept the faith that you will find there. Accept it because there won't be anything else, and because you will know that the absence of anything else is no more a void than death is an ending. You must accept who you are and what has happened to you.*

I put the letter down and closed the door, and went downstairs. I hadn't recognized the name on the letter. Why did I feel that the words should have been written to me? I sat for a long time without moving before I lit the cigarette I'd taken from Father Gerard's room. It was a very expensive cigarette wrapped in pink paper from a box of multi-colored ones: a brand called "Nat Sherman." A few years later, I would pass that tobacco store on a stifling hot day in New York, but by then I would have already quit smoking.

When Sonny arrived the next Saturday afternoon (for his coaching, I thought), he wasn't alone. There was Mr. Perrotti, with a sad-eyed wink for me, and Mrs. Perrotti, too. She was softly crying, dabbing her eyes with a well-used Kleenex, and would not look at me. Nor would Sonny, who kept his hands locked in front of his genitals, like a prisoner in handcuffs.

Mr. Perrotti, like a man with his hat in his hand, asked for Father Gerard. I buzzed the priest's room and led the Perrottis into one of the parlors. Then, before I sat down at my desk, the doorbell rang once more. It was Sandra Czezanski, with her parents, and her face blotchy from crying. She was a short girl with large breasts, in my class at the high school. When Father Gerard came swiftly down the hallway, he herded them into the same parlor with the Perrotti family.

I listened hard and learned that Sandra was pregnant. It seemed very important to everyone that the conception had taken place on the darkened steps behind the backdrop at the last C.Y.O. dance. Father DeCicco was in charge of those dances and asked only that couples refrain from lying down, whatever else they were doing. But it seemed that though Sandra had not lain down, still she had got "knocked up," to use the words of her own father. "That's what happens when you let a guy in a black dress give your kids sex education," Sandra's father said.

Sandra was leaving for Puerto Rico the next day for an abortion. What her parents wanted to know was if she would be able to confess immediately after the procedure and still be forgiven. Her father was a doctor and knew someone down there who would perform the abortion. Her mother was going down with her. And if Sonny ever went near Sandra again, after her return, he would have his two legs broken, Mr. Perrotti offered.

Father Gerard hedged. He said he'd think about it and would provide an answer for them when Sandra and her mother got back. But Dr. Czezanski told the priest he didn't quite understand. They were offering to pay his way down there, to accompany the women, to give absolution to Sandra right there on the spot. A lengthy silence followed. Then Dr. Czezanski spoke: "Aw, Christmas! Will you give the girl a break?"

"I'm trying to think of a way, Doctor, believe me," Father Gerard said evenly.

"Well, try harder. Isn't there some Supreme Court to go to?"

"Well, there's the Vatican, but I wouldn't get them involved if I were you. They aren't known for their lightning dispatch. Besides, they aren't likely to be as 'intrigued' as I am by your sheer audacity."

It was finally decided by Dr. Czezanski that "some Puerto Rican" would be found on the island to absolve the girl.

The Perrottis stayed on after the Czezanskis left. After a while, there was even some laughter, but the voices all were low; I couldn't make out any of the words. Then the phone rang and I had to tell Father Brumley that his reservation for four at Sherwood's had been confirmed, and when I looked again, the parlor door was open and the Perrottis were gone.

The next Sunday, Mr. Perrotti and Sonny walked out on Father DeCicco for the second time. But this was a different item entirely from the walkout on the lecture in the gymnasium. First, this was during his sermon in church; and second, a few other men followed. They all stood outside, having a loud discussion as the Mass continued on inside. Father Gerard went out the rectory door to go over to speak with them, his black dress whipping in the wind. He wore no coat, and he was smiling.

At school, Sonny Perrotti started saying hello to me. "You gonna be my friend now?" he asked. "Sure," I said, walking backwards to my locker, a ridiculous grin on my face. He was holding a clutch purse—Sandra's; she was in a nearby classroom locked in conversation with the somber Sister Bonaventure. I suddenly hated myself.

When Sonny came in for his next appointment with Father Gerard, he slouched down in a chair in my office and asked me how it was going. I told him that I knew about Sandra's abortion. "Oh, that, yeah," he said, momentarily confused, rubbing his jaw, like a prizefighter. "Who told you?" he asked cautiously.

"I heard through the parlor door."

"Figures," he said, satisfied. He hummed awhile, then asked: "You like working here?"

"I like some of the priests. I like Father DeCicco."

"He's a pansy," Sonny laughed.

"No, he's not."

"He's a faggot."

"He's not."

"He's a Commie."

"He isn't."

Sonny stood up and came very close to me, his belt buckle to my nose. Then he pushed his face into mine. I tried to push him away. He caught my arm, but I didn't let up until he did.

The following day, after Mass, Mr. Perrotti knocked out Father DeCicco. One punch was thrown, on the front steps of the church. You're no father of mine, Lester Perrotti, I thought; I called the police. As luck would have it, it was Teresa Masters's husband who responded to the call. No charges were filed. Father DeCicco rested in his room, and Maria Cristina and I took turns bringing him traysful of things that might tempt him to eat.

When, a short time later, Father DeCicco was asked to leave the parish, he did one better: left the priesthood altogether. A black mark on his soul for all eternity; the blackest, in fact, for ex-priests. A few weeks after that, I heard (from the Perrotti sisters, all the louder and larger) that he was living with a woman outside Boston, but the rumor was never confirmed.

Before I left my job at the rectory, the hospital called only one more time to say that someone was dying and wanted last rites. The trouble was, I couldn't locate the priest on call—nor any other priest for that matter. It was on a Saturday night. Who was supposed to be on call? Who? Who? Which one? When the phone began to ring again, I started running all around, upstairs and down, trying to find somebody. Then I stopped, walked slowly back to my little office, smoothed the back of my black skirt, and sat. I folded my hands on the desk, but not to pray. The phone just kept ringing.

# The Eel Man

THE EEL MAN sat on the backrest of his seat, steering the boat with his foot. Collar up, fists hidden deep, he tried to feel again how he had as a kid, sitting waiting for some sweet trouble. Shoulders hunched down against the cold, rounded like a boxer's dodging blows, stiff black hair forked out over his forehead— only his eyes showed from certain angles. Then he let a gull carry his colorless gaze along, as if he were a man out merely enjoying the scenery.

His boat was aqua, painted many times, wooden, stinking with use, but the eel man was not a fisherman nor a sailor of any sort. Until today, the boat had belonged to his father, and so had the name. But the old man had never fished for a living, either. In retirement, he'd won the boat in a card game back at the boathouse, and only after that had he motored around the Sound all day, pulling up from the water what he could, for fun. It was the boys in the boathouse, the father's old cronies, who'd given the old man the name. It was a name from a long time ago—an actual fisherman's name, a nickname—that of someone the boys in the boathouse used to know, or else their fathers used to know him. No one remembered exactly anymore, and now they were trying to pass the name on to the old man's son. They had called it out after him, out of the sides of their mouths, when he'd walked away from them just a few moments ago. The old man was dead now, suddenly.

It felt odd to the eel man to be out on the water at all. He had not been in this or any other boat for years, twenty perhaps. And no one had told him he could take the boat, but there was no one to tell him not to, either. He was going to see somebody.

The eel man leaned around on the backrest of his seat and watched the boathouse shrink behind him. He was already half-way out of the harbor, so the shack looked to him to be about the size of a thumbnail against a fist of rocks.

Inside the shack, the eel man knew, the boys were just as he had left them—slapping down cards on their old wooden crate—and they would still be playing cards when he returned. They would, also, still be drinking—paper cups lined the crate, like watchful birds—and they would continue to drink until it was long past dark. Red cigarette tips glowing, voices rising and falling like those of old men grumbling and crying out in their sleep . . . Fuzzy and Pinhead among them were out-and-out drunkards. The rest were merely lonely in the way that only family men can be. And all of the men were long retired, not from fishing, either, but from jobs they could hardly remember. For forty-seven years, the eel man's father had worked at such a job. In his retirement, the boathouse had been his club.

Before he left to go out on the water, the eel man had paced among the boys in the boathouse, like a warden or a child idle but hoping to look busy or be needed. He did not know why he had come into the place. It held nothing he needed to run the old man's boat.

"Siddown, you're making a wind, ruffling the cards, for God's sake," Winks had said, looking up from his unimpressive shuffling, his eyes watery, his nose red-veined.

"I'm leaving in a minute. Christ," the eel man had said, unsurprised by Winks' gruffness. He knew the boys had no use for him. Still, he did not leave then, but went to stand behind Pinhead's Brother, a soft, squat, round-shouldered man, in a black-and-white striped T-shirt.

Pinhead's Brother cut the deck as if he were a man of importance. Then he turned around to squint up at the eel man: "What are you? My guardian angel? Didn't anybody ever tell you I can't stand nobody standing in back of me while I'm playing?"

"And if you're leaving so quick," Winks closed a runny eye, "why'd you come in here in the first place? Henh? Henh? Why didn't you just get outa your car and into that damn leaky boat?"

"I'm warming up in here. Jesus," the eel man said and went to rub his hands together near the belly of the hissing stove.

Each of the boys trained his eyes on the eel man—all except Fuzzy, who was dealing, his fingers making small, dry-sounding snaps. The eel man had told them he was using the boat to see a woman. He knew they all wondered why he just did not go on his way. The eel man wondered why himself. The stove kettle spat.

When Fuzzy was finished, the boys picked up what they had been dealt and did not look again at the eel man until he cursed them from the boathouse door. And they called out after him, with curses of their own. It was then that they hurled the name "eel man," some of them stroking their whiskered chins, others holding their paper cups aloft.

Riding the rolling black water, past the last buoys of the harbor, the eel man's boat was lifted and dropped by each black wave, and the sounds, like those of a small cannon firing somewhere far off, made the eel man think he heard a salute on shore for some long-lost hero.

He tried not to think about his father. One of the reasons he kept his hands in his pockets was because for some unnameable reason he did not wish to put them where the old man's hands had been; but another, clearer reason was that his own hands reminded him of his father's.

The old man's hands had been so roughhewn. A laborer's hands. The backs of them were the color of tree bark. The palms were crisscrossed with lines, like pieces of a shattered pane of glass.

The eel man took his fists from his pockets and examined them. There were the same square fingernails of his father, but at least they were cleaner. The palms were raw-looking but smooth. But he wished that they were smoother.

He managed the produce department of a large food store, twisting the bright fruits into their places. In the beginning, he had carried the heavy, splintered boxes up from the store's dark, damp basement. Now, a young Hispanic did the stacking on a conveyor belt; the eel man merely stood and caught the boxes at the other end. Still, the eel man longed to work in the office booth on the split-level above the store's main floor, looking all day through the one-way mirror at nothing less than the cashiers' nimble fingers.

The eel man stuffed his hands back into his pockets and made tight fists again. He remembered what he had done to the Hispanic boy that morning, which was why his boss had given him the afternoon off—"to rest."

The eel man had struck the boy after finding the box of tomatoes he had left in a corner of the basement. Rats had gotten to them. Holes had been eaten into the box, and the juices had been sucked.

The boy went out with the eel man's daughter. A high-school dropout, the daughter was sixteen and went now to a modeling school in a shopping center. She had a poodle-ish air about her that said many people had told her she was beautiful, but she was not. And even the eel man admitted this to himself sometimes.

The daughter had not gone to the eel man's father's funeral. The eel man himself had told her she did not have to go, but he had expected her to go anyway. Yet, instead, she and the boy went to the beach in his van. The eel man said: "He doesn't speed, does he? I don't wanna have to peel you off the side of a tree down there." At work he said to the boy: "If I hear you been racing around down there with her, I'll break your head open for you." Since then, the boy had avoided the eel man's eyes and seemed always to be on the verge of laughing when the eel man spoke to him.

The eel man wondered what the boy had been told about him by the daughter. Lately, since the funeral, the eel man had noticed the daughter looking at him with disgust, especially at dinner. He wanted to reach across the table and smack her face, but he did not even say so much as, "What are you gaping at?" He did not want to hear what she might have been told about him by the boy.

Surely the boy had noticed that the many young wives who came into the shop flirted with the eel man shamelessly, outright, as if they thought that to flirt back with them was part of the eel man's job. The eel man had lately come to think that it was, and today he was going to do something about it.

The eel man's old aqua boat sputtered along. The island the town used for one of its beaches edged up on his right. Coursing away from it was the big white ferry that shuttled people back and forth in summer. This trip it was carrying supplies to the old caretaker who lived on the island off-season. Also scattered on the water to the eel man's right were large moored sailboats, all facing the same direction, bobbing into the wind, like giant eyeless gulls.

As the eel man rounded the point, a smoke-colored dock came into view: Mrs. Leland's. He put his boat into idle. The back lawn that sloped up from the dock to the house looked just the way Mrs. Leland had described it in the store—"as tidy as a cemetery." He could see the red sandstone statues of nude women she had boasted about.

To the eel man's surprise Mrs. Leland's house looked rather ugly to him. Its gleaming windows looked broken and jagged, then solid, black, letting no light in, then merely warped and distorting when the late sun hit them in yet another way as his boat drifted by. The current carried the boat into a tangle of weeds at the edge of the property, and here the eel man shut down the idling motor.

His wife would not ask him what he had done on his half day off. There was no question of his being caught. Seeing no sense in hurting her, the boys in the boathouse would say nothing more than that he was out on the water if she ever came looking for him, though the eel man knew she never would. For one thing, she worked—at the Electrolux factory; for another, he knew, if she ever suspected him of anything, she would never do anything about it. What could she do? She always looked so old to him now, moving about the kitchen and bedroom soundlessly in old slippers, like one who knew exactly when to expect the moment of her death and so had no reason to try to outrun it. Once, she was pretty—Miss Norwalk, once—but she had let it slip away from her, like a blanket in the night.

After the funeral, the eel man had screamed at his wife for bringing her mother, and she had stood there, just taking it. Even if the eel man had slapped her, he imagined, she would have merely faltered, regained her balance, and walked away. And he might just slap her yet. He was still angry with her about his mother-in-law's behavior at the church. The old woman was senile, nearly toothless, no taller than an umbrella. And there she had sat before the service, in the private family room, wailing intermittently because she was confused, thinking it was a funeral for her long-dead brother. Every time the eel man walked into the room, the old woman said to him: "You. I seen you somewhere before. Hey," in her broken English, her face turned from the window, pocked and yellow as a cucumber long hidden on the vine, "hey, weren't you one of Bootsy's friends? Hey," pulling his sleeve, "hey, I'm talkin' to you. What's you' name again?"

The eel man's name, same as his father's name, was Joe. But he didn't answer her. He couldn't be sure what might come out, if he'd dared to say anything. There was a lump like bread dough in his throat. He could not swallow it.

As the eel man sat in his boat, he watched for movement behind the wide glass doors that led into Mrs. Leland's kitchen. In the store she joked and touched his shirt pocket and talked derisively of her husband, an eye doctor who was overweight. Daily, at the eel man's stand, she bought grapefruit and celery for her husband, and figs and plums for herself. The eel man was gone from the store between the old man's death and his funeral, and she came to his stand the day he got back and told him she had missed him. She did not whisper, "I'm so sorry," as so many other customers did, but spoke more loudly, more cheerily than ever. "Are these sweet, Joe?" holding a pear to her cheek. "What about these?" pinching off a green grape. And the eel man answered with the refrain he knew she expected: "As sweet as Joe's heart."

Long minutes passed, and still he saw no movement behind the window glass, and the only sound he heard was the lapping of the water against the side of his boat. He wondered if Mrs.

Leland was even home. The house looked empty and perfectly still. He knew he could go up to the house and rap his knuckles on the glass, but he had always intended merely to walk in on her. That was one reason why he had not driven over in his car. He had not wanted her to hear him in the driveway.

The eel man sat and thought about what he should do. Desire was still present in him, palpable as a heartbeat, but so was something else that told him he should go back to the boathouse and face the boys again. When they had been merely his father's old friends, he hadn't thought much about them. Or if he had, he'd felt a little phlegm of disdain rise up in the back of his throat. Now everything had changed. Something needed to be set right between him and them. And he'd see to it. He'd see to it today.

There came shortly, however, the sound of another small boat on the water. The driver of the boat was standing to maneuver the steering wheel. It was a girl with long hair whipping and an arm frantically waving.

She shut the motor off about a dozen yards from shore and let the boat glide the rest of the way to the eel man. She caught the side of his boat with an overlarge, knobby hand, then searched his face, with surprise and disappointment.

"You've got his boat." She tossed a rope of hair behind her.

"'His boat'? Whose boat?"

An eye shut in the pie-shaped face. "You know."

"No, I don't. Tell me."

"Is he up in that house or something?" She poked a chin up towards Mrs. Leland's.

"Tell me who you're talking about first, why don't you?"

"You *bought* his boat, then. He bought a *new* one."

"I wish I could make some sense out of what you're saying. This is my boat here."

The girl muttered something under her breath, then duck-walked back to the stern of her boat. There she began to fiddle with the motor to restart it. The eel man watched her and tried to think of something serious to say. He was being playful only by force of habit. He knew no other way to be with young girls—his daughter's friends and the girls who came to his stand at the store. But he did not feel playful. He wanted to know who was this girl who knew his father.

The eel man took hold of the side of the girl's boat and rocked it. "How do you know Joe?"

The girl turned slowly back around to face him, waited with annoyance for her boat to stop moving, and then and only then answered: "How do *you* know him?"

"We're old friends from way back," the eel man said. "We used to be *very* good friends, in fact, then there was a whaddya-callit, a parting of the ways, so to speak." As he spoke, he tried to drain his face of all expression. The girl was searching it again, this time with suspicion, and he did not want her to see anything there that might make her frightened. At the same time, he tried to study her young face. What he saw was that her lips were chapped or badly chewed, her nose looked as if it had once been broken, and her eyes were olive-black and followed his along.

"Joe and I are pretty good friends, too," she said stiffly when the eel man dropped his eyes to her fingers that were twisting the buttons of her too-small navy pea jacket. The eel man also saw that her wrists, pale as bones, hung out from her sleeves, like the wrists of someone growing much too fast.

The eel man started to say something else, but the girl went back to fiddling with her motor. So he started to scan the floor of her boat. He had the idea vaguely in his head that he would find something there he could use to prevent her from leaving. Everything in this world was too easily lost and never found again; the thing to do was not to let it get lost in the first place. He saw on the floor, propped up between the seats, a stout glass jug filled with a colorless liquid. It was a half-gallon labelless liquor bottle, with a handle. The eel man rocked the girl's boat again, this time more vigorously. "What's in the bottle? A little late afternoon cocktail?"

"I found it floating," the girl said, frowning. "Thrown over the side of a yacht by a drunk, I guess. Or washed away from a beach party. What else? I want to show Joe." She glanced out across the dark channel, as if she thought she might spot the old man, but the water was as empty as the darkening sky.

"So what is it? Gin?" the eel man said.

"I said I don't know. I want to give it to Joe. He'll tell me."

"Give it here," the eel man said, leaning over to reach for the bottle. "I'll take a taste and tell you."

The girl sprang forward and snatched the bottle up and held it to her chest. "No," she said quietly.

The eel man felt something rise up in him; then he calmed himself. "Come on." He drew out the words, trying to sound nonchalant. "What'sa matter?"

"Nothing," the girl said, still in a quiet voice, and with one hand curled around the neck of the bottle, she brought the nails of her other hand close to her troubled face. She might have been getting ready to select a nail to chew on, but her eyes did not leave the hand of the eel man that clung to the side of her boat.

"So, if nothing's the matter, why don't you let me take a taste? You'd let Joe take a taste, but not me?"

"Okay, okay," the girl snapped and with narrowed eyes she held the bottle out to him. The eel man took the bottle with the hand that did not grip the girl's boat and put the bottle between his knees to unscrew the cap, with the one hand only. He sniffed the bottle opening; then he took a burning swallow. "That's mixed martinis in there!" he said.

The girl said nothing. She had moved back to the stern of her boat and was crouched again by the motor. She pulled the starter cord. The motor rattled and coughed, but did not turn over. She pulled it again, and the same thing happened. Three more times, and the motor still did not catch. The girl straightened and glanced back at the eel man. The wind caught her hair and entangled it about her neck. "I've got to wait a minute," she said, shrugging, and with a nervous laugh.

"Here's your afternoon martinis back," the eel man said, extending the bottle to her. "You'll need 'em when you catch up with Joe."

"Oh, keep it," the girl said, with another nervous, high-pitched laugh. She waved the bottle away.

"What am I supposed to do with it?"

"I don't know. Drink it yourself."

"What say I give it to Joe when I see him and tell him it's from you."

"Okay."

"What's your name?"

"Oh," the girl gave another jittery wave of her hand, "he'll know who I am."

"Oh? How's that?"

"He doesn't know any other girls who come out in their boats on the Sound every day, does he?"

"You're asking me? You should be the one keeping track of that kinda stuff."

The girl glowered and turned and pulled the engine cord once more, and this time it caught. A sour smile spread across her face as she moved to the bow of the boat and slouched down into her seat just beyond the reach of the eel man. Her knees in dirty white jeans were parted.

The eel man felt his face reddening. His brain seemed to come loose, bob and float inside his head. His voice, when he finally spoke, sounded hoarse and unnatural as it strained over the noise of the girl's motor: "So you come out on the water every day just to see Joe or what?"

The girl laughed, loudly this time, but the eel man could not be sure if she thought he was foolish to ask such a question or any question at all over the noise. Still, she answered, looking smugly straight ahead at the prickly gray weeds on the shore: "I come out here for my therapy."

"Therapy? What the hell kinda thing is that?"

"I come out here after my work."

"What kinda work? Don't you go to school?"

"*After* school," the girl said. "After school I write. I write songs."

"Yeah? Sing one."

The girl crossed her arms and looked with surprise at the eel man. "That's what Joe always tells me to do!"

"So do you?"

With something like embarrassment the girl looked away again. "Sometimes."

"Does he like any of them ever?"

The girl tossed her head and sniffed. "He likes them *all*!"

"So sing one for me."

"Not in the mood."

"What gets you in the mood?"

"We sit a long time first. Like men. You know. Like men fishing. Like brothers." She giggled coyly, coquettishly, draping her crossed arms over the steering wheel. "And *he* makes up songs of his *own!*"

"Who? The old man?"

"Yup," the girl said, nodding slowly, rhythmically. "And he sings them to me," she added, turning to face the eel man again, with a ready-made smirk, as if the astonishment she must have seen in his face did not surprise her, as if it vaguely amused her.

"Sing me one of these songs of his."

"Can't remember any now. Ask *him* to sing one for you when you see him."

"I won't be seeing him."

"I thought you said you would be."

"Changed my mind."

"You did?" The girl paused, considering, chewing a lip. "Well, then, give me my bottle back."

The eel man stood up in his old aqua boat, the bottle in his hand. "I'll give you your bottle," he said, starting to step boldly into the girl's boat.

Wild-eyed the girl began to scramble. "What the hell are you doing?" With a yank of the steering wheel, she reeled her boat around and threw the eel man off balance and backwards into his own boat again. When he had picked himself up, he looked and saw the girl speeding away, a gray explosion of water trailing behind her.

Sitting on the floor of his boat, the eel man felt wave after wave of shame sweep over him. He could not see over the rim of his boat to the shore, but he could see Mrs. Leland's still dark, empty house on the hill—it seemed to be hovering just above his head as the late afternoon sun lowered down—and the sight of it, so close, increased his shame. This was not where he should be. He had no business here, he had no business on earth at all. The whole landscape that surrounded him seemed alien, a place he didn't belong, and never had, a place inhabited by strangers, now more than ever.

When the smell of liquor reached his nostrils, he knew the bottle was broken, and this, for some reason, was what finally made him feel his grief. He found the bottle's jagged-edged neck and with a dream-like, almost casual gesture, he cut into his palm with it carefully, slowly, intricately, pausing occasionally to look up, not in pain—he felt no pain—but as might a man writing an only half-thought-out message on a slip of paper. Then he played with the wounds from which ran bright strings of red.

The eel man sat numbly until darkness came. The darkness seemed to give him strength. He went to the stern of his boat, moving dizzily, like a dreamer just waking, and he started the motor.

The old aqua boat had no lights, but the caretaker's house on the island beach did, and they seemed to light the eel man's way. Some of the large moored sailboats had lights, too, hanging in triangles all along their masts, and some of the whale-sized rocks were lit, and the buoys bobbing on either side of the entrance to the harbor. And when the eel man got inside the harbor, instead of going slower, he speeded up; and he knew that when the boys heard the sound of his boat and went to the door of the boathouse and called his name, he would answer them.

# Sounds of the Rude World

F LOOD IN INDIA. Good," Abdul said as Anna guided her
bike into the office. He was reading a newspaper headline
to himself and eating a hamburger for breakfast. Both chubby
brown hands held it up to his purplish lips like a religious offering. He sat near the door at a low, gray metal desk that was
piled with papers and looked too small for him. His soft, round
knees must have hit its underside. Abdul was the bookkeeper
as well as receptionist at *Model Aviation*, but his frequently stated
ambition was to become a U.S. government accountant. Three
nights a week he attended the Benjamin Franklin School of Accounting on K Street, a few short blocks away.

Anna parked her bike against the wall behind him, on which
there was a huge framed poster of a man hang-gliding out across
a placid sea. The photo was a blowup of a miniature, and the
man was made of plastic.

"Pakistanis hate Indians," Abdul instructed Anna. She seemed
to need a lot of instruction. If he had met her on a dusty street
at home, he would have pegged her as a lost one, but at least
she had the gift of knowing she was lost. Some people were lost
and did not know it. They didn't bother to go looking. Unfortu-
nate occurrence. On the other hand, Abdul himself no longer
searched. He hoped to become a practical man, an American.

"Why do you hate them, Abdul?"

"We hate each other," Abdul smiled.

Anna shrugged and took a hairbrush from her knapsack. She began to brush her dark veils of hair. Her desk was in a tiny office off the reception area, but she liked to spend a little time each morning with the peculiar Abdul. So far he was her only friend here.

She stood behind his swivel chair and read the paper over his shoulder. She gasped, pointing to what caught her eye: an obituary on the crowded front page. Someone famous had died. "Oh, no! I loved him!" She held her hands in the prayer position under her startled eyes and read a brief caption under the photo praising a long life well-spent.

"He made cars?" Abdul looked puzzled and not altogether approving of the fuss.

"No, *mobiles!*"

"Oh, I know what they are. Machines."

"They aren't machines."

"They are mechanical, mathematical. I know how they work."

Anna said nothing more about it, but asked to borrow the section of the newspaper that carried related stories and reminiscences. In her office she would read the details of the artist's life, trying each on for size, like coats on a rack in a store. It was impossible that all the facts would fit, but Anna always hoped that they would.

Abdul peeled away a section of the paper and handed it back over his shoulder. In exchange Anna would listen to him brag and complain. Abdul was a constant reminder to Anna, who had just enrolled in an acting class, that some people in the world were still content to pursue a modest American success.

"How did you do on your accounting test, Abdul?"

"Got B!" he told her proudly, as if there were no grade higher. He wiped his mouth with a folded handkerchief. He had just finished his hamburger in several small swift bites. "And how is your jumping going on?"

He referred to Anna's stunt job. Every night for a week she had been playing in *Tosca* at the Opera House. ("For 30 seconds, so don't bother coming," she had told him when he had expressed some interest; anyway, she couldn't get anyone free tickets.) For $25 a performance. Padded to look twice her size, she leapt from the parapet of the prison-castle of Sant' Angelo to her death below onstage.

"Tonight's my last night to do it. I'll miss it."

"You don't get hurt at all?"

"A little. I do have a few black-and-blue marks," she said with both hands busy making a braid.

"And some day you will jump and sing both?"

"Oh, no! Not me. I don't want to sing. Unless I have to, to get a role or something."

"I like you, Anna," Abdul said in a confiding tone, as if he were admitting to a fault. "But I worry for you. I wish you luck. The kind of success you're after is very, very hard to obtain."

"But it's not the 'success.' It's the doing. There's something about it that pulls me up straight, makes me feel like a real person, not just a mess of little details ready to explode in a thousand directions."

Abdul held up one creased finger, by way of telling her it was his turn to speak. He got his wallet out and showed her a photo of a little girl cupped in his palm like a charm. "My wife works washing other people's hair, you know. She makes $4,000 a year plus tips. We have this child, five years old, still in Pakistan, living with my wife's parents. And until my wife and I earn enough to send for her, in Pakistan is where she will stay. It is we, we who have exploded in a thousand directions."

"I'm sorry, Abdul," Anna said weakly.

Facts, no more, no less, Abdul seemed to say by his steady grimacing gaze. With the same fixed expression, he changed the subject: "Ramadan is coming," and he would have to fast. He would have to get up in the middle of the night and eat a meal of fried bread. And he was somehow gleeful in his pronouncement, so sure was he of the ways that the universe chooses to work, even in Washington, D.C.; so proud, but pretending to be annoyed by the demands it places on the faithful. And they may not have been the best of friends, Anna and Abdul, but they liked each other well enough for co-workers. And if, by some chance, they became enemies, it would come as a surprise to Anna. Abdul, with his heavy black eyebrows evenly drawn over dark, watchful eyes, observed her freely, unabashedly as she got her messages out of her mailbox and headed with her bike down the hall. The ways of Americans which appealed to him, he adopted; others, not. Hamburgers, yes, religion or not. Thanksgiving turkey, never, he smiled. And his lips were very wet, slightly opened—he used a great deal of saliva when he spoke, as if he meant to say much more, then stopped himself.

The lights of Alex's tape recorder danced, obeying his music. The room was lit up as if for surgery. Very important work going on here, the lights said. Some people of influence agreed. And his parents' money had bought him a New York debut at Carnegie Hall last year:

> *Alexander Longley, a pianist and composer, whose interesting background includes studying to be an engineer and a fling as a rock musician, last night displayed the willingness and digital ability to investigate composers as diverse as Scarlatti and Alkan. His own compositions, "In a Small Plane, Flying" and "Suite: Anna," were agreeably buoyant. . . .*

Alex made strange breathing noises when he practiced. He was aware of nothing outside the music. His beard at midnight often would still be matted from sleep of the night before, but his nails were perfectly trimmed, his hands pure white and womanly smooth. He used a potholder to lift even a tepid coffee pot to fill his cup.

At the office coffee machine Anna poured herself a cup and looked at the bitten nails of one of her hands. She never did learn to take care of them properly. Wasn't a bride-to-be supposed to grow her nails, outgrow childish habits? A Bandaid was wrapped too tightly around her thumb. Just this morning she had cut herself clumsily slicing a piece of bread. A dot of blood was on her sleeve. She rolled the cuff and headed towards her cubbyhole with her steaming coffee.

In the hallway Anna met up with Harold, the business manager, who gave her a lecherous grin. Overlecherous, the forced grin of impotence, Anna had decided early on. *Heterosexual panic,* a clinical term came to mind today. She had learned it the other night, reading idly in a book of psychiatric definitions she'd found in one of the bookcases at Alex's parents' house. Alex's parents had moved to Florida. Alex stayed in their house rent-free. And so had Anna up until three weeks ago. Alex had three pianos all in one room, two grands facing one another, and an upright against the wall. Piano books, record albums, and tapes were piled everywhere, shelves of them sagging with the weight. Once Anna herself had studied to be a pianist, practiced all day, wrapped the sounding board with a blanket, so she wouldn't disturb her neighbors. Gave herself a two-cookie reward every hour.

It came to nothing.

"How are you, Harold?" Anna asked without looking up at him. She already knew what he looked like with his pants hiked up too high, his alcoholic slenderness.

"In what respect?" Harold replied, laughing through his nose.

Sometimes, when his eye caught hers, he quickly made his lips form a kiss. "Think I'll turn queer and blow this place," he said every evening to Anna, poking his white crewcut into her office as he prepared to go home. Anna laughed the first few times, out of a nervous politeness. Now she knew better. But Harold wasn't discouraged. And neither was she. She had a little notebook, lined and spiral-bound—a child's plaything—and into this she had written the yearly salary she'd been promised, dividing it into monthly, weekly, daily, and hourly portions. Looked at from those perspectives, the money didn't seem like such a huge amount, but Anna didn't let it bother her. The job—the money—had allowed her the freedom to be on her own for a while. Now if only she could do what she had set out to do: become someone.

"Are we going to see you on Johnny Carson one of these nights soon?" Harold asked.

"Not too soon."

"Why not? You're going to be famous, aren't you? Can I have your autograph?"

She knew he meant well, but it was hopeless. Finally she smiled. That seemed to be all he wanted from her this morning. He pinched her arm, then weaved down the hallway.

He was a former military man and somehow gave the impression that he was still in uniform; probably his posture did it. Anna had been led to believe, when she was a child, that to succeed in life all one needed was to hold one's spine straight. But here was proof of the opposite. Harold's wife had committed suicide a few years ago, Abdul had told Anna. He'd never remarried, and his drinking seemed to worsen daily. This explained him, made it easier for Anna to accept the sloppiness with which he handled life. Abdul had not only accepted Harold's ways, but had worked them to his own advantage. He suggested Anna do the same. The time to ask Harold for raises, Abdul told her, was after, not before Harold had been to lunch.

Passing through reception again, Anna saw that Joan had arrived. The secretary to the publisher, Joan sat at the desk next to Abdul's, hunched over an enormous pocketbook. Anna carried her coffee past her, saying good-morning but not stopping to chat. Conversation flowed unnaturally between them. Anna kept going down the glaring orange carpet to the safety of her office.

Joan's permed head was lowered as she routed in her bag, but her eyes were raised and followed Anna, fixed at the level of her waist. Joan put her elbow down onto the desktop and let her wrist fall.

"Annaaa," Joan sang playfully. "Mama's got a surprise for you."

Anna was wearing her new green fake velvet jeans with the rhinestones on the pockets. Turning to face Joan, Anna suddenly felt foolish in them—Joan was staring. Anna smiled quizzically. She was a little afraid of Joan. The pocketbook on her lap gaped open. "Hi. What?"

Joan slowly rose from her seat to reveal the same star-studded tops of her own green fake velvet jeans pockets.

"Oh, no!" Anna laughed; they both did. And each said yes, yes, a good buy—on sale—at Garfinkel's. But at the same time the coolness could be felt by each of them. Anna had understood from the beginning that the two would be civil enough to each other, but never friends.

Joan's face was rockhard, even as it laughed, with sharpened features. She made the fake velvet and the rhinestones look, not lighthearted, the way Anna made them look, but garish, cheap, like an off-color story told by a woman about a woman. Joan paraded around in front of her desk, striking poses.

She looked as if nothing could harm her. Studying her, Anna had the chilling idea that she was foolish to believe that she could ever be up on a stage. She did better at hiding. Joan could probably get up on a stage with ease if she wanted to and take what would come and give a handful of something back, maybe, right in the teeth of the audience. And Alex was made sturdy enough for the stage, too. He would be the pianist of the family—if they ever did get married. He would be the one to face the sea of glinting eyeglasses waiting, blinking, coughing. He would be the one to sit at strange pianos, each one long and shiny and black as a hearse.

"Aren't you committing suicide nightly for money?" Joan asked in her husky voice, so certain of itself.

"Just one more time left: tonight."

"Doesn't it make you feel creepy?"

"Yes, but it also makes me feel more alive afterwards. It makes me want to live my life and a few other lives, too, if possible. It makes me think: Now last night that could have been it. And I wouldn't have seen this day and the fact that you bought my same pants. That's worth living another day for, I guess."

"You don't sound totally convinced."

"I don't? Well, I am. I think I am."

But Joan had finished listening.

Abdul was telling someone on the phone that on his tax returns he always put down $200 in charitable contributions even though he never contributed anything to anyone. "They don't check," he explained to his friend, "unless it's *over* $200."

All day Anna heard Abdul on the phone, talking to his friends. She didn't mind. She liked to listen. It seemed to be a lucky mistake that she had this office, this job as editorial assistant at all. She did know something about grammar, punctuation, stylistic consistency. Once she had been quite serious about poetrywriting. It helped. Anyway, she could do the work, which was mostly looking for other people's errors. She had been given a long strip of copy to proofread at her interview. She found every mistake, aided by the fact that she knew the terminology, being familiar enough with Alex's hobby: flying real planes.

Anna turned to her work, today's strips of typeset copy waiting to be read word by word, letter by letter until their meanings fell away to nothing. That was her proven method of proofing, and so intent upon it was she that it might have been that her eyes moving down the page were correcting all the little errors of her own life. At the end of a page, she raised her head, and the newspaper she had borrowed from Abdul caught her eye. She opened to the obituary and read the review of the life of the man who had made such beautiful things, things difficult to ignore. How wonderful to be so enshrined, to walk through your life with such sure steps. But of course one would have to be a genius. The night she'd quit piano in despair, she told Alex: "But I'm not a genius! And I just don't think it's worth it if I'm not going to be the best!" "What about me? Am I a genius?" Alex retorted. "Yes!" Anna cried out and watched the pleasure forming on his face.

When she heard Abdul talking to Douglas, the publisher, just outside her door, she quickly put the newspaper away.

Like Abdul, Douglas had a wife and child—two children, in fact—but unlike Abdul, he didn't have to worry about money. He'd been set up with the magazine by his father, who had made a fortune in D.C. real estate in the early fifties. Douglas knew nothing about running a publication and he freely admitted this, as if it were a point in his favor.

Abdul told Douglas the news of his test grade. "Fantastic!" Douglas said, and Abdul repeated the news to get another, more sincere, more considered "Fantastic!" out of him.

Douglas, so content to be himself, Anna thought. Some mother somewhere must have told him he was It. Otherwise why did he wear that perpetual grin? He sauntered into Anna's office, looking overconfident, leading with his hips. He was moderately good-looking, but in a spoiled schoolboy way, and he loved to hang around her.

First, he stood by the window, looking down at the 14th Street strip joints and porno shops. The office address was on the much more respectable 15th Street side, but the suite itself was on the backside of the building. So much else of Washington was sand-blasted stone and immaculate as a cemetery. Four-teenth Street was all hot-pink, eggy-yellow, trash flying everywhere. A neon sign above the doors of one of the strip joints blinked alternately, "This is it!" "This is it?" It was not a well-kept secret that Harold went there every day at eleven for his two or three martinis— and a beer for nutrition.

Douglas talked to Anna about bike-riding. He lived nearby her in Georgetown—he, in a grand home on tree-lined Q Street; she in the tiniest efficiency above a Greek carryout on noisy M Street. Anna carried her bike down a long dark flight of stairs every morning, with the crossbar on her shoulder. At the front door, which was flush with the sidewalk, she braced herself. Once she stepped off the sidewalk and joined the rushing traffic, there was danger. Cars seemed to carry her with them; buses bore down behind her. She could not go her own way—she had to go with the flow of the traffic.

"I thought I saw you fall this morning," Douglas said, jingling the change in his pocket.

"Not me," Anna said guardedly.

"A girl that looked a lot like you was cut off by a taxi. She was sprawled all over the place with her skirt up over her head."

"Glad to say it wasn't I."

"I know it wasn't you—I stopped to see if it was. You don't think I would have kept going if I thought it was you lying there hurt. It worries me that you ride a bike. You could take a ride with me. I go right by your place."

"You don't always come in," Anna said evasively.

He came closer towards her, took his hand out of his pocket, the one that had been jingling the change, and touched the top of her nose.

Anna recoiled, but he persisted: he pulled her ear and whis-pered into it, "You know, if you finally do get to know me, you won't find that I'm any better than this, but at least you'll never find that I'm a worse person than the one you see right now."

Anna opened her mouth to say something—she didn't know what—but Douglas was shaking his head to stop her. He gave her ear another tug, and left the room.

The pigeons resting underneath her window air-conditioning unit were cooing. In Boston, where she and Alex had gone to college, two pigeons had made a nest in a planter on their apartment balcony. Sometimes Anna and Alex would see the pigeons down on the sidewalk outside their apartment building. Friends doubted that they could tell one pigeon from another, but they knew they could. Neither Anna nor Alex had ever liked pigeons before that; then, eventually, they watched this couple hatch their eggs.

She got up from her desk to take a closer look at the birds. If the job included sleeping with Douglas, would she do it? Never. She tried to think of one other thing she knew for sure, and failed.

"You know my wife's job is far more demanding than mine," Abdul was telling someone on the phone. "You know how they let me go here and there, whenever I like. . . . She doesn't drive. It takes her forever to get there by bus from Arlington. . . . In Silver Spring. . . . She washes the scalps of American women. . . . She thinks of them as her children, that's how. . . . Yes, she hates them sometimes. Other times, she is in love with them, hopelessly, wanting to be them. Sometimes she wants to kiss their fingers, their toes. . . . Their faces are not beautiful, she tells me, but they are real—you can touch them: that is the important thing. She is not afraid to touch them. She can tell that some of them are afraid of her at first. . . . She wins them over, and then they beam up at her, with their heads turbaned in towels. . . . Sometimes she cries while making dinner. . . . First, I say stop that, sternly, reminding her that she must be strong. But she keeps crying, so that I see that my scolding doesn't do any good. In fact, it's doing harm. So I comfort her, with her head in the crook of my arm."

Anna was listening to Abdul so intently, imagining her own

self as somebody's wife, she was startled enough to jump when Joan came to her door. She asked Anna if she wanted to go to lunch and help her look for a tennis outfit afterwards. She was signed up for an indoor course this fall and winter. "We seem to have similar tastes in clothing," Joan laughed. She had her big black purse slung over her shoulder. Anna was too surprised at the friendly invitation to say anything other than yes.

They ate some yogurt, stirring it up as they stood at the newsstand across from the Treasury Building. They sampled the fashion magazines and *Model Aviation*'s competition. Then they went around the corner into the high-ceilinged Garfinkel's. Anna liked being with Joan, much to her surprise; she even liked that they were dressed alike. It made their outing seem somehow official.

They flipped through a rack of tennis dresses on the hushed sixth floor. Anna saw in the lighting that Joan was not so young. She had assumed that, like herself, Joan, too, had just graduated, but apparently not. Abdul had hinted to Anna of a serious flirtation Joan was having with Douglas; in fact, he had implied that it was something more. Anna tried to read in Joan's face the extent of the truth of this report.

Joan tried on three or four of the dresses, then some skirts and tops, modeling them all for Anna, who watched Joan watch herself in the mirror. Joan gave even her own reflected image that same I-dare-you stare. Quickly, decisively she made her choice—a white, pocketed tennis skirt with a maroon polo shirt and maroon socks.

They strolled around in other departments, like old friends shopping. They started walking back to the office when it was time. Then, waiting to cross at the corner Anna spotted Alex up ahead at the next crossing. His back was to her, and for a couple of seconds, she sized him up as if he were a stranger. She was attracted and glad that there were still some decent looking men left in America. Then she realized who it was.

"Joan! I don't want to see Alex, and he's right ahead of us. Probably he's going up to the office. Do you mind going back by yourself?"

"Who? That guy with the beard? He's cute."

"Yes, you go back. I'll call you from a pay phone, and you could tell me when he's gone."

They both watched him stride up the hill past the Treasury as the light changed. He was wearing a burgundy muffler around his neck, even though it wasn't at all cold out. Anna knew this meant he could not work. It meant he was going flying: the muffler, the leather jacket, the torn corduroy pants were all part of his superstitious aviator outfit in any weather. He owned one-quarter of a four-seater plane parked at a Gaithersburg airport.

"Let's both hide," Joan suggested brightly. "I don't feel like going back yet anyway. We can call Abdul and he'll tell us if Alex is gone. And you can tell me why you're ducking around corners, afraid to see your own fiancé."

Anna said nothing, but they both took off, two young women in forest-green pants, zigzagging through the lunch crowd.

They walked up 14th Street, fearless together. Darting into a doorway, they spied on Harold walking down the street on the other side of the block. He must have been returning to the office from "This is it!" At the end of the block, he paused to talk to a man and watch a young black woman walk by. The woman was well-dressed, haughty looking. Both men watched as if she were alive and so expensively groomed for their pleasure alone. Anna couldn't see the expressions on their faces, but she could see their heads slowly turn as the woman passed. After she crossed the street, the men resumed their conversation. They looked quite alike; both had the same haircut, anyway. I have always envied men their conversations with one another, Anna suddenly realized. She and Joan hurried away so that Harold wouldn't see them.

"So are you going to tell me why you're hiding from your Alex?" Joan asked over the noise of groaning buses.

"It's nothing too mysterious," Anna replied. "I think I don't want to be married to him after all. But I haven't told him yet. This is the first I've admitted it, even to myself."

"Engagements are broken off all the time," Joan mused.

"Are they?" Anna asked hopefully. She tried to believe that Joan was a good source for that kind of information. She felt as if she were moving down the sidewalk of a foreign city, things were so different. She'd never been walking on this street before. She'd only driven it or seen it from her office window.

They walked in silence, past windows blocked with paint and paper to hide what was behind them. Customers made quick, deft entrances and exits; only proprietors lingered in front of these store fronts. Eyes followed Anna and Joan, but Anna, for one, didn't want to turn back. She felt protected, with Joan by her side. And she didn't want to see Alex. But she couldn't walk forever. It was getting to be a very lengthy lunch hour. Finally it was the forthright Joan who suggested that Anna stop at the next pay phone and make the call to Abdul.

"Is Alex there, Abdul?"

"He was here and now he's gone."

"How long ago did he leave?"

"Ten minutes."

They hurried back to the office, Anna ready to dart around a corner if she had to. "But what's the big deal about seeing him?" Joan asked, out of breath now as they trudged.

"If I see him, I'll love him," Anna said simply.

In the golden lobby, in the middle of it, there was a seedy coffee shop and a newspaper stand. A man sat there all day with a hat on, smoking cigars. He wouldn't let Anna read the magazines—he wouldn't let anybody read them—but Anna took it personally. Near the stand they found not Alex but Douglas, who called Joan over to have a private word with him. For once, he wasn't smiling. Joan obeyed, and Anna went up to the suite alone.

"Long lunch today," Abdul said, glancing at the clock when Anna walked in. Seated in one of the reception-area chairs was Alex, nervously batting his chest with his scarf.

Anna glared at Abdul, thinking: he may as well not have any legs, he's always sitting there watching everything.

Alex followed her into her office. She stood at the window, looking down at where she just had been. She held onto the windowsill, bracing herself as if for a blow or a vibration of the building. She couldn't remember what season it was, and whether they were going into or out of the cold.

"Come with me this afternoon," Alex whispered into her ear.

"I can't, I can't," she said, staring ahead.

"Tell them you're sick to your stomach, threw up all over your desk." He pulled her close to his side.

"Can't, can't," she repeated.

"Will you come over tonight?" he said.

She said nothing, just sighed, thinking: he's drawing me in, even as I resist. I used to pay such close attention to him, thinking something might be revealed, something important, something told just once. I had the distinct impression I was going to learn something about myself.

"I love you and I need you to practice the orchestral part of *Rhapsody* with me.

"I'll come," Anna said. "But it'll be late. After *Tosca*."

After he left she went out to confront Abdul. She just stood in front of him and stared. He was holding the photo of his little girl. "Civilization often progresses as the result of lies, my friend," he said, and his purple lips, outlined in black, were perfectly smooth.

She walked out of the office, headed she didn't know where, maybe to harass the man with the magazines downstairs. Impatiently she waited for the elevator down, but when the doors opened, she didn't get on, because out came Douglas, then Joan, who was sobbing into her hands. When she saw Anna, Joan ran for the stairway while Douglas continued down the bright orange carpet to the office, a deaf man. Anna followed after Joan, who threw herself onto the floor of the stairwell. Her sobs echoed loudly. Anna sat down beside her on the cold cement and patted the back of this stranger. Joan sat up and fell into her arms. Anna sat comforting her, feeling the wetness of Joan's tears soak through her blouse to her chest. Neither one of them had a Kleenex. Joan had only a little calendar in her great big black purse. She tore pages out of it and blew her nose with those. There were tissues in the ladies' room, but the ladies' room was locked. Abdul had a key, but neither one of them wanted to move from this spot.

"Once, I went to one of those swinging clubs with him," Joan said through subsiding tears. "To meet another couple, maybe. We almost went to a party, but I chickened out at the very end.

One of the men came up to me—I'd never seen him before—and touched the tip of my breast. Now the idea of it sickens me.

"The first time Douglas came on to me, I didn't see how I was going to get out of it, so I did something really dumb: I asked him for money. At least I could get that much out of it, I thought. He wrote me a check. It bounced! My bank charged me $15 for a returned check fee. It ended up costing me money."

Joan laughed bitterly, holding shut eyes that looked as if they burned. Anna laughed, too, half-heartedly, thinking: are these the only kinds of secrets that women have to tell each other?

She remembered she had told so many of her secrets to Alex, her deepest ones. Of failures, embarrassments, and cruelties she'd been guilty of. And she had told him stories of other people's failures, and he, growing uncomfortable, had told her, in turn, it was not necessary to divulge too much, some things were best left hidden. But Anna went on anyway, soothed by the sounds of betrayal, by the very sounds of her own voice.

"Just once," Joan said, "I'd like to be introduced as 'Joan Gordon, Brain Surgeon.' Except that then I'd probably want to go back to being Joan Gluck again. 'Gluck' sounds much more brain surgeon-y than 'Gordon,' don't you think?" This time the two young women laughed genuinely, and couldn't stop laughing for a while.

Then, after they had sat for several long minutes in silence, Joan stood and smoothed the starry pockets of her pants. Anna could see that she felt better. She expected Joan to say that she was ready to go back to the office. Instead she told Anna that she didn't want to be left alone. Could Anna be with her all night? Could they get out of here right now? Could Anna just come with her? Anna said yes.

She went back into the office to get her knapsack—she'd leave her bike here overnight—and began to think of things she might say to Joan, things she should say to herself: "You know you can still love men without hating yourself." That was the most important thing. Then she thought: we all have these powers over each other, and most of us don't know the first thing to do with them.

She put away into folders the galleys on which she'd been

working. It could all wait until tomorrow. And if Douglas fired her? Fine. She knew she was going back to live with Alex, anyway. One of the pigeons took off from the ledge, catching her attention. Much more of a miracle than a plane. Off the side of a building, flying, not falling like a rock or a suicide. Passing once more through reception, she did not say good-bye to Abdul. Anyway, he had his ear to the universe: "Got B!" he was telling someone else on the phone. "B!"

# The Motorcycle Riders

T HE TIRE BLEW, and we swerved across the three lanes of
traffic. Reed tried to steady the bike, but we zigzagged
crazily. The road had turned to butter under us, and I thought:
So, it's finally happening— the thing always in the back of my
mind finally coming forward to be faced. And I was elated.

The bike let us down gently, like a camel falling to its knees, for
we were no longer going very fast. Then we toppled, and my
helmeted head—clunk!—hit the black, sparking pavement. It
was night. I can still remember the silence when the motor shut
off. Reed was under me, the fast lane under him. And with that
sudden realization, my peaceful feeling was replaced with a
fright so palpable, it blocked vision, memory, everything, everything but will.

I crawled off to the median strip, the corners of my mouth
stretched by a ridiculous grin. No, it must have been faster than a
crawl. Then a different kind of calm and peace filled all the space
around me; it must be like what mountain climbers feel when
they finally reach the summit. I knew I was safe. Then I was
lifting my cheek from the grass to see that Reed was going back
for the bike, and I was telling him to leave it where it was, very
calmly, as if to say: "Leave the dishes, I'll do them later." (How
could he do this after we were both safe? I could see so clearly
what different, separate people we were.) He pulled it off the

road, over the curb, and onto the median strip with us. It was a small bike, tiny really, but as he struggled with its weight, it seemed impossibly huge, and he, laughably, smallest of all.

The grass must have been dewy, but I didn't notice. A picnic sort of mood came down as I watched people run towards me. How crowded the world must be, for these nice people to appear out of nowhere! Cars had stopped, both those we had almost hit and those that had almost hit us. A middle-aged black couple and a young white woman with perfectly tweezed eyebrows reached me first. I remember her eyebrows very well. I knew mine needed attention. We had frightened her and the black couple. They were excited, asking me if I was all right. I was alive, wasn't I? I wanted to say, so what could the fuss be about? Yes, I think so, I replied. My voice was far away, and I couldn't stop grinning.

The black man helped Reed wheel the bike across the highway, so he could chain it to a tree. Meanwhile, I discovered that my right arm, the one I'd fallen on, felt rubbery, but only someone very ungrateful to be alive would have mentioned it, and so I didn't. I suddenly knew how important it was to be orderly, polite—I'd seen something hidden by the thinnest gauze, and how strange it was that I had been emboldened by it.

The woman with the perfect eyebrows, like croquet hoops, got back in her car and drove away. Where was she going? It was late. I wondered if she were going to meet a lover clandestinely. Then the black couple offered to take us home, and we drove with them through the city in their enormous car.

It was very dark inside that car, after the glare of the highway and the airport lights (for that treacherous stretch near the airport exit was where the blowout had occurred); and the stereo speakers behind our heads were of the highest quality.

Did this couple find it strange to have a pair of passengers now? Their car seemed intimate as a bedroom—weren't we intruders? They were acting as if our unexpected company was a pleasant surprise. I was unspeakably grateful for their generosity.

The woman smoked, and had a smoker's husky voice; Reed bummed a cigarette (wasn't this asking too much?—evidently not) and we all talked about the accident as if it had already happened a long, long time ago.

I felt a gripping, a tightness, just below my waist, at the top of the hipbone; a stinging, as if I had been burned there, in that spot only, by the sun. I saw Reed touching himself under his shirt at the same place. Was he hurt? He couldn't be; he was alive. But as we got out of the car in front of our row house I saw under the glare of the orange street lights that his shirt and shorts at his hipbone were stained with dots of black.

People with a moment in common, we said our good-byes and thank-yous to the couple—never enough. Then, slightly sheepish (how foolish we had been, tempting fate, wearing summer clothes, on this hot August night on the highway), we turned to face our neighbors, the Muellers. A young couple, like us, in their twenties, they were sitting on their porch drinking beer.

"Want to buy a motorcycle?" Reed asked them, smiling.

"No." A question without the question mark, from Bill Mueller in his undershirt. They both waited to hear what we would say next—for we rarely spoke to them. This was, indeed, a very special night.

"Just got dumped off it."

"Somebody hit you?" Cheryl Mueller asked, leaning forward on her kitchen chair. She sounded ready and eager to blaspheme any driver who would do a thing like that.

"Tire blew."

"Front or back?" Bill Mueller asked.

"Back."

"You lucky it wasn't the front," Bill Mueller pronounced, satisfied with himself and such a sturdy piece of wisdom.

"I'm glad I don't ride no bike," said Cheryl Mueller, folding her arms and looking off into the orange-lit night, and I felt my foolishness freshly.

Inside the house, Reed lifted his shirt to reveal a red gash. Already, however, the blood he had spilled was dried, and now it looked painted on, theatrical. I asked if he would mind walking the dog, because my foot was cut, my sandal broken, though my hipbone was merely bruised; it had not bled at all, and I felt a sudden, stupid stab of envy. Why hadn't we been hurt equally? Why the difference even in that? Then I remembered the exact configuration of the fall: I had been literally cushioned by Reed, who, in turn, had had nothing but the pavement to land on.

I went upstairs and got undressed and decided to take a bath. The tub wasn't dirty, but I wanted to scrub it anyway. The only trouble was, I couldn't think of what to scrub it with. The sponge must have been right there, under the sink, but instead I used a clean washcloth from the linen closet. I was proud of the neatness of that closet, though Reed thought such fussing was a waste of my time: procrastination in disguise.

I ran only about an inch of water and got in, and because our bathroom is in the front of the house, I could hear Reed outside talking some more with the Muellers. He sounded jovial.

When he came upstairs into the bathroom himself, he took off his shirt to look more carefully at the gash in his side, and the color drained from his face. His whole body turned greenish-gray—as the color drained from the skin into the vital organs (he would explain to me later, for, once, he had taken a course on treating accident victims, given by the Red Cross). He dressed his wound, then treated himself for shock: feet up, head down. I was very impressed. We both lay in bed—awake, not touching, like a traumatized honeymoon couple, or strangers forced to share the same mattress. We did not comfort each other during the night—nor did we speak. We lay awake, hardly even moving, until morning.

At five-thirty, I got up and went downstairs, and ironed table-cloths I'd been meaning to iron for the past two years (we had used them at the wedding party we'd given for ourselves). But my right arm still felt wrong. I turned on the radio, softly, and a song I liked came on, but I found that I couldn't snap my fingers. My thumb seemed sprained. Could I still write? I got a piece of paper and pencil, and with some considerable pain I printed:

*One should be spilled off a motorcycle at night onto the fast lane of the highway—and crawl off to the sweet, soft grass of the median strip, with just some cuts and scratches to show for it—at least once in a lifetime. But no more than that.*

Then I just kept signing my name.

When Reed came downstairs, he no longer looked ill, just groggy—and determined: he was eager to get busy attending to the rest of the details of the accident's aftermath. He called his office, told them he wouldn't be coming in; called our doctor; then as he ate dry raisin bran out of the box he called his friend Keaton and asked him to help him pick up the bike, using Keaton's big green camper. I was amazed! Who cared about the bike? Cars were abandoned; why not motorcycles? I never wanted to see the thing again. I had known all along it would come to this. How right I had been! And it was only sheer good luck that the accident hadn't been much worse. But I wasn't going to say a word. The lesson was learned, and we wouldn't have to speak of motorcycles again.

An hour later, they were wheeling it into the garage behind our house.

"It's a hurtin' pup," Keaton said in a mock country voice, then hurriedly left, late for work, while Reed assessed the damage. The bike's headlight was smashed, a foot pedal twisted around (the reason why my sandal had broken, and why my foot had been scraped). Also, the cycle's license plate had been stolen during the night it had spent chained up.

"Well, anyway we'll sell it now," I said.

Reed said nothing, circling the bike.

"But, then again, would you really feel right passing along our bad luck to someone else? Maybe we should just push it over a cliff."

"Luck? This is a piece of machinery."

"Yeah, and look at it."

I knew I'd never ride on it or any other bike again. That was for sure. That was my choice, just as I had freely chosen to ride when Reed first got it, about a year before the spill. The year's duration—it seemed important. It seemed portentous. Or it should have as the first anniversary of owning the bike had rolled around; now, of course, it was too late—I should have thought of that before.

At noon, we went to see our doctor, who told us we had hairline fractures, and that Reed probably hadn't gone into shock after all. He'd merely been badly frightened and only later let himself feel its full effects; if his body had needed to go into shock, it would have done it sooner—back on the highway, for example.

This doctor had a gray mane, and an Argentinean accent, so

"hairline" came out sounding like "c-c-c-hairline," and "have" like "c-c-c-half." During our visit, and examinations, he took several phone calls from his frantic wife; men had been hired to chop down some trees on their property, but neighbors on all sides of them were complaining.

"Tell them they are air trees," he whispered into the phone. "Nobody c-c-c-helse's." Then, more loudly: "Toler-c-c-c-hance . . . toler-c-c-c-hation!"

At the end, he apologized to us for the interruptions, then took it upon himself to lecture us about cycles, and tell us how lucky we were. I kept agreeing, while Reed glumly smiled.

That evening, to relax, we went to the movies. It was horrendous, trying to park downtown—sometimes like a parade, other times, a chariot race. On any other night—before the accident, that is—we would have taken the cycle and pulled into a snug crevice right in front of the theatre. Reed, grumbling, rounded the block again. We drove around and around it in our hulking car.

"At least we're alive," I said to Reed's grimaces.

"Who said we're not?"

At the end of the month, as planned, we went to see friends on Martha's Vineyard. On the way we listened to *Huckleberry Finn* on the car's tape deck. Life seemed good. My thumb was healed, though my leg was still covered by ugly black-and-blue marks, turning greenish-yellow (these bruises had shown up later). Our other wounds would take much longer to heal. And every time motorcycle riders went by, I couldn't help but point and comment on the fools.

Reed was irritated by it, and finally told me so: "When you're in the car, you're in a box. On the cycle you're sky-diving."

I told him I'd never felt like that. (Except on the night of the accident, I reluctantly reminded myself.)

"That's because you'd never let us go fast enough. If you go fast, you're not really aware of the bike under you. It's you flying through the air without any help at all. It makes you feel as if you can do anything."

I told him the only time I'd felt freedom like that was when

I thought I was going to die. Otherwise, I'd always been scared to death.

"I always feel the opposite of fear. For moments, I don't believe in death at all."

"You're crazy."

"Don't say that."

"Why not? It's true."

"What makes it true? Just because you think it's true? We can feel different ways about things. I don't tell you you're crazy to do some of the things that you do."

"Things like which?"

"Never mind."

"Tell me. I want to know."

With a cramped fist he drew words in the air.

"It's not life-threatening, Reed."

"I'm not saying it is."

"It's my business. I'm not giving it up."

"Of course not. I wouldn't want you to be any saner than you are. I hate sanity."

"Thanks a lot."

The friends we were visiting in Chilmark were fairly new ones. They were staying in a family summer house, a screened-in cottage high up on a bluff. And the first thing they told us when we got there was the one house rule:

*"Don't slam the refrigerator door!"*

It was gas-fueled, and the pilot light could easily get blown out and would have to be relighted, which was described as "a pain." But it was even more of a pain, they said, if the light went out without anybody noticing.

When I slammed the door the first time, Felicity sank to her knees to check underneath the thing to see if its little blue flame was still burning. It was, and we smiled like sisters; but throughout the weekend, I kept slamming that door. I never learned. Luckily, the light never did go out on me. Each time, I got down on my knees, and I always saw the little flame flickering in the dank and dark.

Lots of other relatives of my friends were also staying nearby on the bluff. There were a number of family summer homes connected by paths in tall reeds and bramble. You could meet up with a huge Golden Retriever, whether or not you took a wrong turn. There were three of them, a mother and her sons, and I learned all their names very well, and called them out as I went along stealthily.

The dogs belonged to Felicity's brother, Mark, who was a lawyer; a cousin of hers was a young intern; a third relative was studying at the Wharton School to be a banker; and Felicity herself was a chemistry teacher at a prep school—waiting for motherhood: sane ones, all, who liked their gin and tonics and loathed tackiness above all other crimes.

"And fat people," said Felicity's husband, Dwight, who raised funds for the school where she taught. "I hate fat people. Don't they know they're killing themselves?"

One night, it was somebody's birthday, and we all ate lobsters spread out on newspaper on the living-room floor: a strange and pleasant picnic. There were lots of colored balloons blown up. We batted them around. Then someone remembered something people used to do in the sixties: lie down on balloons. Anyone of any weight could do it: lie down on a line of balloons. If the balloons were held steady by many helping hands, and if still others lowered the stiffened person down, the balloons wouldn't break.

So we tried it, starting with the littlest, somebody's ballerina of an eight-year-old. And it worked. I was lowered down next, 115 lbs. Five people held the balloons. Five others held me, and I lay for a few moments on a wobbly set of firm balloons, feeling as if I were on top of a giant spring. And it wasn't so much fear that the balloons would break, but that they would shoot out from under me, or that I would roll off them. Everyone assured me. Then Reed tried it, 145 lbs. He was lowered down, and lay on a bed of balloons without breaking them. Everyone of every weight tried it, and the balloons didn't break. Then two people together: Reed and the little ballerina, for instance, standing on his chest.

On the beach that afternoon, the two of them had made sand castles, sand people, sand dogs. The fog had been so thick that you could not see anyone beyond your blanket. As one of the real dogs walked away in the fog, I couldn't see his feet. Then he disappeared completely. It was a private beach, so there were not too many people on it anyway. But if you strayed too far, you could lose even the friends you had come down with.

The weather throughout the evening of the birthday party was like that. The fog made it impossible to see out the windows of the cottage. It came right up to the window screens and rolled inside.

"What do you think of Dwight?" I said close to Reed's ear as we lay in our separate sleeping bags on that living-room floor, the fog circling in around us. "Don't you think he thinks everyone should be just like him?"

Reed didn't reply. "Reed?"

"Reed," I whispered more loudly. But he was already sleeping. And I felt the way I always feel when I learn I'm only talking to myself.

Then I listened for the sleeping sounds of the rest of the people in the house. And I must have thought of the night of the accident. For months, even the slightest discomfort could call it to mind—particularly the jubilant aspects of it—and I always wondered if I would ever feel anything quite like that again.

When we got home from our vacation, Reed discovered why the bike tire had blown. He'd replaced the inner tube incorrectly: human error—a hunch he had suspected—not bad luck at all. So, calmly and without castigating himself, he changed the tube, fixed the headlight—got it all ready, in fact, to go back out on the street.

Would we sell it now? I dared not ask the question aloud. For one thing, it was none of my business.

The next day, Reed got a new license plate.

I watched from the porch as he rode away, hunched, elbows out, on rims of air.

# From a Juror's Notebook

> Overheard in a jurors' ladies' room: "I'm glad
> I don't have no rape trial to sit on. Man
> accused of rape? He guilty. He accused,
> that's enough for me."

I SHOULD FIRST OF ALL record here that we are not allowed
to take notes while in the jury box. Perhaps the court would
frown on this notebook, too, but that kind of prohibition (disal-
lowing any writing, even in the jury's own waiting room, the
place where we will eventually make our decision) would be
absurd and unenforceable.

From memory, then, I will give you the rudiments of the trial
so far.

In the courtroom I'm glad I'm not seated near the front. (I
am Juror No. 8 and sit in the back row, out towards the end.
We're probably seated alphabetically, but that's a guess. I don't
know my fellow jurors' names.) The farther from the defendant
I am, the better. I hate when he looks me in the eye. He looks
at all us jurors squarely. Unafraid. (Has someone instructed him
to?) He seems gentle, on the one hand; on the other, he seems
dull-witted and capable of bumbling into violence. He would
feel sorry, but he would have an excuse, something justified by

laws of his own. Why does he strike me as a man who keeps his word? *His word.* I haven't even heard him speak yet. (And we may never: he isn't required to; it is neither his nor his lawyer's job to prove his innocence. The other lawyer must prove his guilt.) I suppose, then, that I think of him as a man of his word because he is so silent, lips closed tightly: the secret truth is his. And all I have for now is my imagination busily working.

The accused—and how much more is he assured a cell at Lorton simply by being labeled as such?—is a black man. Clary Wright, built like a football player despite his ethereal first name, is charged with robbery, burglary, rape, sodomy, forgery, and uttering. What is "uttering"? Will I find out? I can only guess that it is howling, hurling, sputtering, spewing words in a public place. And I must admit that I myself have been guilty of that upon occasion.

Clary Wright's alleged victims are a young couple living not far from me, on a street very much like my own—lined with town houses of multi-colored brick, flat fronts, common walls between them, front doors that open directly onto the sidewalk. Step out your door and you're on the street, out in the world, and so had better be prepared for it.

I had half expected Clary Wright's victims to be white, like myself, but they aren't. Alfonse Harrison, a keenly dressed black man in his early thirties, claims that one night he was walking from his parked car to his front door when Clary Wright and another man Clary will identify only as "Cheese" walked up behind him, put a gun to his back, and forced him to enter his own home. Veronica Townsend, Alfonse's "common-law wife" (in court, "living together" has no precise meaning), and their one-year-old baby were upstairs in the master bedroom. Veronica was watching TV while her baby nursed.

That is how it began, according to the prosecuting attorney, Mr. Salazar, who spits his words like a mediocre drama student. Tall and thin with flexible knees, elbows, and wrists, and silver-framed glasses that contrast sharply with his very black skin, young Mr. Salazar also informs us that Alfonse was once himself in Clary Wright's position in the courtroom—that is, the accused. He was once convicted of armed robbery, but has straightened himself out, and now works for the mayor as a community organizer in his neighborhood.

Mr. Bledsoe, the other lawyer—fiftyish, squat, baggy-suited, with mocha-colored skin—paints quite a different picture. In the cadences of a preacher he says he will not only prove his client's innocence, but will also show that Clary Wright is an acquaintance of Alfonse Harrison. Mr. Bledsoe announces, further, that Clary Wright did not steal Alfonse's gold necklace and gold Gruen watch—items Clary was wearing when he was picked up by the police at the bus station where he worked as a security guard. Nor did Clary steal the money order which Alfonse bought to pay his mortgage and which, instead, Clary cashed after affixing his own name and an approximation of his home address. These items—necklace, watch, and money order —Mr. Bledsoe smiles, were *given* to Clary by Alfonse in reparation for the bogus cocaine which Alfonse sold and Clary returned on the night in question.

We were told to go home early yesterday afternoon and told to report back this morning. And so we, obedient ones, sit around the conference table in our long, windowless room, without speaking. We aren't permitted to discuss the case, and have nothing else in common—not that we know of—and any conversation two or three of us might engage in would be heard by everyone. Which wouldn't be awful—only awkward. So, instead, we are silent, the violet fluorescent lights buzzing overhead, everyone staring into space, except me (writing, very tiny, into this hand-held notebook), and except for the one I call the Black Nixon, who is reading a hard-backed book the title of which I cannot determine. The dust jacket is missing. Has this jowly, stern-faced man left it home on purpose?

We are dressed up as if for the office—or for church. The men, especially, are shined and spruced, except for the lone white male, who has a scruffy beard and bushy eyebrows (like a youngish, and very angry, Santa Claus). He wears chinos, a white shirt, and ill-chosen boldly printed tie (black and red—a modern, swirling, somehow hostile design). He keeps batting his chest with the tie, and glaring at the wall. The newspaper on the table is his, but he leaves it untouched. A minute ago, when he saw me looking at it, he offered it, gruffly, but I just as gruffly refused. In fact, we often look antagonistically across the table at one another. If we were to strike up a conversation, much less a friendship—to say nothing of a relationship!—how obvious! We are the only two whites on this jury. And yes, we do have the color of our skin in common, but I am determined not to acknowledge this, and by his cold-eyed glances I can guess that he feels the same way. And yet I do want to speak to him. I'd say: Aren't you glad that both the accused and the alleged victims are black? That way, when finally our discussions do come, they will necessarily be free from any racial overtones. Won't they? I am so determined to be impartial, a somber, sober member of the citizenry about to engage in a serious task.

I am a desirable juror, for this case, I guess: 30-year-old free-lance writer. That's all the lawyers know about me: age, occupation. That and what I look like—sauerkraut-colored permanent growing out; white, makeupless face; small frame, with flat chest; in dim light, could pass for high school senior. They also know my *yes* or *no* answers to their questions asked *en masse* during the jury selection process. For example, "Has anyone been a crime victim in the last six months?"

All those who had been victims lined up to whisper the details to Judge Clarissa Hightower—a regal-aired, pale-skinned black woman (yes, both lawyers *and* the judge are black, and so, as it were, cancel each other out). With an unseen hand, Judge Clarissa turned on and off a "noise" machine (which made a sound like a wind blowing, a small localized storm) for privacy during each consultation.

The lawyers alternated asking questions of us seventy-odd potential jurors for an hour or longer. The bearded juror—I'll call him the Beard—went up to the bench repeatedly to confer, a terrible scowl on his face. Apparently he had been a crime victim; had strong feelings about gun control; would be offended by the explicit details of a rape trial; would be offended by mentions of guns and drugs; would perhaps give more credence to the testimony of a police officer than that of an ordinary citizen; would perhaps, also, give less credence.... A man of principle,

I presumed, I, who did not raise my hand once. Curious, and also bored from the waiting, I *wanted* to be chosen.

Did any of us have trouble hearing? Anybody? Anybody? That was the final question we were asked. An old white woman dressed in black raised her hand. She was ushered to the front, using her black umbrella for a cane. Judge Clarissa's noise machine went on, and she shouted above it, saying she might be able to hear, yes, if they'd only just shut off that blower.

When the real picking began, it felt distinctly like sports team captains were making their considered selections. (One more reason why I wanted to be chosen?) When it was over, and we'd taken our assigned seats in the jury box, and the unselected ones had been sent out of the chapel-like courtroom and back upstairs to the jurors' lounge, the lawyers looked us over again, worriedly, as if they were displeased with every one of us, had made a terrible mistake—twelve mistakes (plus two alternates). Nonetheless, there we sat, with everyone—judge, lawyers, marshall, bailiff, court reporter, and defendant—all just looking, not saying a word, as if *we* were the ones on trial, we in our box with only one exit. As if they were waiting for *us* to say something now.

\* \* \*

Day Two: I look around the table. People have made friends, somehow. People are talking. Someone's daughter is getting married. Someone else is on a bowling team. The Black Nixon has paid $2,000 in taxes out of his salary already this year. The Beard has brought in an *ARTnews* magazine, but he isn't reading it; he's just holding it up, pretending to read. He's watching everyone around the table instead. Including me.

Alfonse Harrison finds it laughable that Clary Wright would claim to be a friend of his. He also laughs at Mr. Bledsoe's claim that he sold drugs out of his house.

"Why would that be impossible?" Mr. Salazar asks his client.

Because it was, Alfonse replies, a house where the community met. "And the community would not put up with it."

But there seems to be something missing from his answer.

For it also happens to be true that Alfonse was once convicted not only of armed robbery but sale and possession of drugs.

But that, Alfonse says, was a long time ago. Now he is a "product of rehabilitation," a "success" living in a renovated townhouse his parents willed to him, a house he speaks of as his "kingdom."

Which kingdom, he says, was violated by Clary Wright and the absent, vanished "Cheese."

Nor does Alfonse hide the fact that he wanted to find the two men and kill them, "because that's what any man'd do if the same thing had happened to him."

What happened was this, at least according to the witnesses for the prosecution:

Clary Wright and "Cheese," after putting a gun to Alfonse's spine, marched him through his own front door, forced him to strip, and tied him up, his hands behind his back. Alfonse lay naked on his living-room floor, with his "bum hanging out," while Clary, who held the gun, and "Cheese," described as smaller and darker than Clary, ransacked the house, stuffing whatever they judged to be of value into green plastic garbage bags.

Upstairs, "Cheese" discovered Veronica, raped her, and forced her to sodomize him, then made her take both him and Clary on a tour of the house, pointing out objects of value their own eyes might otherwise have missed on their preliminary accounting. When they finally left the house, they had the necklace and watch, and, a few days later, Clary cashed the money order at the bank on which it was drawn, using his real name and address, though he did transpose a couple of numbers.

Why had six weeks been allowed to pass between the night of the crime and the day Veronica talked to a California policewoman about what had happened to her in D.C.? College-educated, slim, thirty-two, Veronica is cool on the witness stand. A very fair-skinned black woman with long straight brown hair, she, like Alfonse, is extremely well-dressed, in a below-the-knee, lavender wool skirt and matching cardigan sweater. Quite plainly cool, she answers all the questions about whether "Cheese's" penis was indeed inserted into her vagina, inserted into her mouth. She breaks down only while recounting how it happened that "Cheese" spat her own breast milk into her face. Remember: moments before the attack, Veronica had been nursing her baby, who lay on the floor while the rape was in progress.

Mr. Bledsoe is cocky, almost jovial, with all the other witnesses but Veronica. These others include the arresting police officer, tall, handsome, black detective in a navy blue business suit; the bank teller, pretty black young woman with her hair in ringlets, who sold Alfonse his money order; the bank teller, slim young black man, who cashed the money order for Clary, dressed in his guard's uniform, his cap pulled low; the girlfriend Veronica stayed with after she fled her own house and before she left for California.

The girlfriend's red dagger fingernails, snaky red dress, and vampire makeup made me wonder. Maybe she and Veronica have known each other since childhood?—these two women who seem to have nothing of appearance (except skin tone) in common. Or maybe Veronica has radically altered her style for court . . . ?

At any rate, Mr. Bledsoe was playfully cynical, flagrantly doubtful, about the veracity of this parade of story tellers. All the witnesses seemed to make him see the comic side of life. He even succeeded in tricking Alfonse into admitting that yes, true, many gold necklaces in the world resemble one another and this one tagged as evidence may, in fact, not be his, after all—though the Gruen watch bears his and Veronica's initials. . . . So Mr. Bledsoe has been pleased by his own performance, until, that is, it comes time to play opposite Veronica, who looks him squarely in the face and gives the same straightforward answers she's given her own attorney. This makes Mr. Bledsoe fumble for euphemisms (". . . did his bidding," for example)—flabby, undramatic phrases Veronica does not find it necessary to substitute for the real ones.

Initially, Veronica admitted, she lied. She told authorities that *both* men raped her—to make the crime seem worse, to make the police work harder in trying to capture them. But when Clary, who had *not* raped her, was the only one brought to trial, she, understandably, changed her story.

So, if "that faggot there," as Clary was termed by Alfonse,

was not the one to rape Veronica, why is that one of the charges against him? As Clarissa, our queenly judge, would explain, a man can be accused of rape if he merely "aids and abets" in the act, without actually engaging in it himself. This aider and abettor "is just as guilty" as the one who does the raping.

Whatever the letter of the law, it doesn't change the fact that there is a lie mixed in with the truth. Are there other lies perhaps? For example, *did* Alfonse sell drugs? And did he get into some difficulty with Clary Wright and "Cheese"? And did it turn ugly, so ugly that Veronica became a victim? And did Alfonse then vow to find the men? And did Veronica leave him and vow not to return until the men were ciphers?

If so, then Alfonse, himself formerly a man of the street, had no choice but to go looking for the violators of his kingdom; then, failing, desperate to get back his love and his baby, went to the police for help, knowing that his word would be believed over that of accused rapists.

I wonder.

I also wonder if Alfonse's and Veronica's relationship was suffering difficulties before the night of the crime. Veronica did leave Alfonse, going to live with friends on the West Coast. She ran from the house, hysterical, on the night of the incident and refused to return. Either Clary or "Cheese" had left his raincoat behind, and when Veronica saw it, she started screaming, and couldn't stop. Alfonse burned the coat in the fireplace, trying to make her stop. But it didn't work. And she fled.

The raincoat burning is a detail that pleases Mr. Bledsoe very much. Burning potential evidence? Why? What were they trying to hide? "If we had that coat here right now," laments Mr. Bledsoe, "we might have asked Mr. Wright to slip it on, try it on for size." It is conjecture which makes Alfonse glum, for as he explains once again, he burned the coat because it was making Veronica scream her lungs out. What is more, Alfonse had no intention then of sitting in a courtroom about this matter. Burning the coat was the last thing he did before going out and trying to find the two men and commit murder. And when he couldn't find them after several weeks, and with Veronica seemingly not in the least tempted to return East, Alfonse did finally go to the mayor himself, not only his boss but a personal friend since Alfonse's rehabilitation, and ask the mayor to ask the police to start an investigation.

Which led, by means of the money order he had cashed, to one Clary Wright.

How willing I was to give the benefit of the doubt to Clary Wright! How much more I preferred a crime of passion to one of random violence! Recognizable! But as sure as I feel that Veronica and Alfonse have told a skewed story, I also feel sure, after listening to his own testimony, of the guilt of Clary Wright.

He has a soft voice. What a surprise! He has a wife and daughter, too, he says.

How old is his daughter?

"Fourteen," his answer, is greeted with sharp laughter in the courtroom. He has just said his own age is twenty-four. Is he mistaken? Or *did* he become a father when he was ten?

It *is* a fact that he worked as a security guard for one of the bus companies, and was issued a gun, which he was allowed to take home on weekends. We are shown the application he filled out for his job at the terminal, and are told to note his lie about having graduated from high school, for in truth he did not go beyond the ninth grade. We are also given the details of his prior conviction for bank robbery—admissible, as was Alfonse's record—so that we may better evaluate him as a witness.

Down at the police station, Alfonse and Veronica both picked him out of a line-up with ease. They also picked his photograph out of a stack of glossies.

But that's because they knew each other from drug-dealing episodes—Mr. Bledsoe stresses.

Well, then, does Clary, by any chance, wish to reveal "Cheese's" real name *now*? For he might be brought in to corroborate Clary's story.

But no, "Cheese's" real name has escaped Clary.

And his address and phone number?

No, he can't recall those, either.

How did they get together with each other, then, as friends do?

Clary just sat in the parking lot of a housing project on the edge of D.C.

Where?

He forgets where.

He just sat there, hoping it was the right night and hoping, doubly, that "Cheese" would step out of the shadows and hop into the car, so they could drive into the city together and "score" some coke, hunh?

"That's right," says Clary.

Mr. Salazar accuses Clary of not even knowing what cocaine is. "He's heard that football players take it," he tells us jurors, his spindly legs strutting. "And he's trying to be cool, making up a story like that. But I'll bet he can't even tell what weights it comes in or how it feels to take it."

Is Mr. Salazar right?

Clary just sits there, his large hands clasped, finally not using his soft voice to say anything at all.

It's nearly the end. Mr. Bledsoe recites poetry for his final statement. The word "Nay!" keeps repeating. None too subtle message. He holds up one finger each time, like a Roman orator.

Then Judge Clarissa reads us all the laws and sections of laws we'll be discussing. "Uttering," she explains, is to put forth as genuine a counterfeit document—in this case, the money order that belonged to Alfonse. And she takes special care with the rape law, pronouncing very distinctly the aiding and abetting part of it.

\* \* \*

I stopped writing last time when a marshall came in and told us to pick a foreman. Our choice looks just like the policeman who testified. He is also the tallest, handsomest, and best-dressed man in the room: fortyish, well-spoken, in a navy-blue suit, he was already sitting at the head of the table before our choice was made.

The foreman has been given a piece of paper on which to make our collective marks: Guilty, Not Guilty. All counts but two are painfully easy to decide. We look around the table at each other and sigh. There is little discussion, except to reassure a couple of the older women. One wonders where Alfonse got all that money for a "relevated" house. (She means "renovated.") The house was left to him by his parents upon their deaths, we remind her, and she seems satisfied and embarrassed for bringing it up. It bothers another woman that Alfonse and Veronica aren't married, especially since they have a child. The issue, however, seems to everyone else to be highly irrelevant to the guilt or innocence of Clary Wright.

But the rape. And the sodomy count. There is grave disagreement over these.

"I, for one, have no difficulty seeing that a man who goes with another man into a home to commit crimes is guilty of all the crimes that get committed in that house that night," I say. "Especially if that man is the one who holds the gun, as Clary Wright did."

Several of my fellow jurors agree with me. Several others, however, do not see it that way at all.

"He didn't do it!" they shout.

"Aiding and abetting," we shout back.

But then they point to the piece of paper on which there is no place to check "Aid and Abet." There is only "Guilty" or "Not Guilty."

The foreman, the Black Nixon, and the Beard are among those who will not vote "Guilty."

The foreman says, "Too many black men have gone to jail for rapes they did not commit."

But the law states, we counter, that *even if he doesn't actually do the raping, he's just as guilty as the one who did.*

"Well, I don't believe that," says the foreman.

"Well, I don't think we're here to say what we believe and don't believe," I say. "We're here to implement the laws as they are written." And I'm surprised by my own insistence, by my desire to do what the law requires. How I cling to this!—something written, something we can know for sure.

"You're probably the kind of person who took one look at him and said, 'He's guilty,'" the Black Nixon says to me.

"You're wrong about that, you're just wrong."

The Beard gets up from his seat then and paces around the

table, saying, "My father was a prosecuting attorney. He regrets things now. He saw injustice played out again and again, and he was a prime party to it."

"But we're not supposed to be judging the laws," I say. "When you agree to be a juror, you agree to play by the rules, to go along with the system."

"Who agreed?"

"You agreed."

"But I tried to get out of it!"

"But you didn't."

Everyone starts talking at once—to anyone who will listen. I say, "Stop! How can anyone think? This is complete confusion."

"It's part of our heritage—talking all at once—you know," the Black Nixon says to me.

How can I reply to a statement like that? I say nothing.

"What happens if we can't agree?" someone asks.

"Hung jury."

"What does that mean?"

No one knows for sure.

Could Clary Wright be sentenced only for the crimes we can settle on—and let the rape and sodomy charges go?

That would be the same as "Not Guilty," we "Guilty" voters protest.

We must decide on them all.

Veronica Townsend could go through the trial again with another jury, someone says.

But is that true?

"You gonna make that girl go through all that again?" one of the older women who wants to vote "Not Guilty" asks me. "How's that gonna make her feel?"

"How is she going to feel if we go out there and say, 'Not Guilty'?" I ask. "*She's* the one who's pressing charges. *She's* his accuser, not me!"

We decide to ask the marshall, sitting outside the door, to ask the judge to reread to us the rape law. As always we line up consecutively, and file out into our seats in the courtroom once again. To my surprise, the lawyers are in their places, too, and so is Clary Wright.

Does *he* understand the laws under which he is being tried? Pondering this, I make my crucial mistake: I look directly at him at the moment that his eyes are staring at mine. His are hooded by dark brown lids; the eyes themselves are a shineless black, as if made of fur or cloth. They look as if they might stare into mine forever, and I feel the blood in my veins leap ahead harder— back to, or away from, my heart. I look away quickly—as quickly as I can—but it's too late. Eyes don't lie. They know what they have seen: Clary Wright has told me something. He has said that he has the truth, while I am only guessing. Friend or foe, he was there in that house that night. He knows everything.

I look to Judge Hightower. Has she seen Clary Wright's face, too? No, she is too busy delivering the words of the law with annoyance, impatience, this second time. She shouts "aid and abet" and "just as guilty as if . . ." We all file back into our hateful jury room, chastised.

We glance sheepishly around the table at each other. We decide to vote again, anonymously. Slips of paper are torn from this very notebook. When these are counted up, there is still one holdout.

"All right, who is it?" we all demand. "Who is it?"

Afterwards, I went to the cafeteria with the Beard, whose name is Simon. I have told him my name, too. We really didn't feel like eating, but there was no place else to sit and talk. What we felt worst about, we both readily agreed, was the defense attorney's insistence that we all—not just the foreman—stand up and say out loud "Guilty," "Guilty," "Guilty"—everyone of us individually, up and down the rows. I did not look at Clary Wright as I spoke the word—I looked schoolgirlishly down at my wringing hands—but I stole a look later. His eyes were silent black rocks glowing with anger and something more I dared not name.

Simon glumly bought a little salad. I got an ice-cream sandwich. We took a small table in the crowded seating area. Absently, he reached over and took the napkin of the woman sitting at the next table. She gave him a cold, rude stare. I recognized her as a marshall I had seen in the hallways; besides, she was wearing her badge on the pocket of her army-green blazer.

We tried to explain to her that we were jurors, both very shaken—we'd just convicted a man.

She just kept staring.

And because there was nothing else to do—he certainly couldn't have given it back to her, could he?—Simon finished dabbing the napkin over his lips.

# Keepsake

NANCY TRIED TO USE her old key, but found that the lock had been changed. That stung. Did these people think Nancy and her family couldn't be trusted? Did they think the Ouellettes would walk right back in whenever they felt like it? Nancy had waited this long, hadn't she?

She pushed the yellow point of the doorbell—a slim girl, with a full moon face, wearing jeans and an overlarge jacket. So many other times she had been on the inside hearing the bell, not outside ringing it. She waited and rang again, and still her friend Gretchen didn't answer. Probably Gretchen was scared—she was baby-sitting in this house tonight—but Nancy had told her that she'd be coming over.

Nancy followed the cement path around to where she knew she could reach a window. She pulled back some barberry bushes planted by her father.

"Ouwwwwchshit!" A thorn pierced the pad of one finger. She sucked at the pinpoint of pain, probably no bigger than a shaved whisker. A fleck of black pepper. If she could have seen it in the dark. Yet how it hurt! But that was nothing compared to the pain she'd suffered lately. She shook this puny pain off and looked in the window. She could see Gretchen standing there. Nancy rapped her knuckles on the glass, and Gretchen reeled, her hair in wings, made with a curling iron, her earrings, three in each ear, dangling like tinsel on a tree. Nancy shouted: "It's me, it's only me!" hating how her voice sounded dead, thrown back at her. And she hated to have to go through all this to get into the house she used to call home.

Gretchen came to the window, her thighs rubbing together in flesh-colored stretch pants. Her wings fanned a thin face that Nancy envied, hollow-cheeked, with a small white knob of chin; but there was nothing else thin about her—the exact opposite of round-faced Nancy, who'd lost weight besides, during her recent ordeal. An interrupted pregnancy. But didn't a thin face show its worries more plainly?

"I'm going around to the front, let me in for God's sake," Nancy said, pointing with her hurt finger.

Gretchen said, "Ohmygod!" and she and her thighs disappeared.

As she waited for Gretchen to come open the door, Nancy sucked in her cheeks. That made her face look more angular, anguished with love, or sex anyway; at least that was what she hoped—most times, nobody was fooled. But she was only trying to look less babyish, less like she was ready to believe anything anybody told her. She turned and waved to Mark in his darkened car at the curbside. It was small, Japanese, a blue that the sky never was, and dented everywhere, not by careful Mark, but by a previous owner. It looked like crinkled paper, not metal. Nancy held up five fingers. Brent, her old boyfriend, wouldn't wait even that long. Mark probably would wait forever, but Nancy didn't want him to freeze. She'd told him to let the motor run; she'd even pay for the gas; she had no money, but Gretchen always did.

What "things" had she left behind? Mark had asked before they got here, with his filterless cigarette burned nearly to the end, though he kept it in his mouth anyway. His bottom lip was often blistered by hot ash. In the darkness, Nancy had seen neither a blister nor the rest of his face, but she could smell the cream he spread thickly over it. Acne had shot his face full of holes, which he tried to cover up with the pumpkin-colored cosmetic. His whiskers grew unevenly over the scarring. "What 'things'?" the glowing stub had repeated. And that time Nancy could hear that he was poised to be jealous. So she'd assured him that the stuff had nothing to do with anyone else. (Meaning Brent.) And it didn't. She'd been worried about "something" during the move, she said (not mentioning the pregnancy); that was why she'd left it all behind in the first place. It was in the attic crawl space. That was why nobody else in the family had seen it and packed it up. Souvenirs; some dolls, a Snoopy. And a diary. Which she didn't want anyone reading. Especially not a stranger. She hadn't kept the diary long; it might not even bear her name. And it didn't have to do with boys. But she wanted it back anyway.

When Gretchen finally opened the door, Nancy walked right in past her. "God! What is *wrong* with you? How could you not know it was *me*?"

"I thought it was you, but—" Gretchen hung her head and the trios of earrings dangled down. Her sister, a nurse, had done the piercing for Gretchen, but Gretchen had done Nancy's. With a needle and ice cubes. One lobe almost got frostbite: it turned white and brittle as dried dough, which anybody might have snapped off only by touching it. But Nancy had forced Gretchen to keep going, even though they both heard the sickening squeak the needle made. The the holes got infected—they oozed and crusted. And Nancy was trying to let the holes close up, so she could start over again.

"I hate baby-sitting, we're too old for it," Nancy said. She had walked farther down the front hallway, to look into rooms; then she stopped, unprepared to be as amazed as she was. How could anything look so different? Suddenly she felt invisible, like a ghost must feel, roaming around in the future. She didn't belong here. Yet she knew it all so well. It felt like walking around in a dream: home—what could be more familiar?—yet here it was all askew. For one thing, the wall-to-wall shag carpeting was gone. Her heels tapped on bare wood floors, except when she walked on the squares of multicolored rugs strewn around. Shiny wood furniture stood on those rugs. The legs of one table were polished and gorgeous as a horse's legs. Nobody slopped around in these rooms. There was nothing frayed or waiting to be re-placed. No junk. Probably no junk drawers, either.

"I don't believe it!" Nancy said. "My grandmother used to have her chair right over there!"

Mrs. Auclair, with her nose hooking down to meet her lips, as if it had melted like wax, couldn't even dress herself toward the end. Nancy remembered her in the chair, lapping up soup with her furry tongue. But Mrs. Auclair had left the house not just to Nancy's mother; it was a gift to all her four living children. The house couldn't be divided like a cake, though; it had to be sold and the money split. And Nancy and her family had been forced to find a new place to live. Nancy's mother no longer spoke to her brother and sisters as a result of it. And Nancy didn't blame her, though at the time she hadn't cared. The move had come during the weeks when she thought she was going to have Brent's baby.

Nancy walked from room to room, saying, "Innnncredible!" And: "Unfuckingbelieecceevable!" Gretchen said nothing, because she had never seen the inside of this house until tonight. Nancy and Gretchen hadn't become friends until the pregnancy. The friendship happened not only because Gretchen would listen to Nancy talk for hours, mostly in the girls' room at school, cutting class. Gretchen's sister the nurse was the other reason. She'd know the right people to call for an abortion—if it came to that. And Nancy would have gone through with it if she'd had to; people did it all the time. And then it happened that she did want the abortion, because Brent wouldn't agree to live with her—and Nancy said she'd be damned before she'd raise that child alone! But Brent had no money for an abortion, he said, even though he'd just bought four new radial tires. And Nancy certainly had no money. If she didn't have any for a jewelry-store earpiercing, would she have it for anything else? Still, the baby continued to grow, nothing to stop it—until the miscarriage. A bloody emergency, right in the second-floor girls' room. And Nancy had actually seen the baby she'd lost. And so had Gretchen. And they agreed they'd never forget the sight for as long as they both should live.

"If you could have only seen it!" Nancy kept saying, making Gretchen feel, as usual, left out. She was talking about the house. In the living room wine-colored drapes were looped around window frames. The Ouellettes' dusty venetian blinds had covered those same windows. On the bookshelves, where the Ouellettes had only had clutter, this new family had put little objects—carved men and dogs and other strange beasts of perfection. Nancy's eyes smoothed them as with fingertips. They smoothed everything in the room, including upholstery, which looked like closely grown flowers, tiny, mossy ones of all colors. "Like whad-dyacallit? Baby's tears? Or baby's breath?"

Gretchen just kept examining herself in mirrors, which Nancy said were in places that had never had mirrors before, and the places where Nancy expected to see herself were blank, painted surfaces. Nancy pointed them out. But Gretchen was wondering out loud what she would be paid for this evening. She wouldn't know until she got home, because she never had the nerve to look at the wad until then. There was never a set fee. She took what was given her.

"We're too old for baby-sitting other people's babies," said Nancy, but she wasn't even listening to herself. She was looking at all the golden light in the room—like a fireplace glow, but the only light was coming from lamps. Did this family use the fireplace a lot? Nancy's hadn't.

"And what's that smell?" said Nancy.

"I don't smell anything," said Gretchen, sniffing like a rabbit. Still, there was a damp, clean odor: potting soil. The house was growing in corners; plants cascaded down ledges, crept along the mantle, like they'd been growing there for years. Nancy stuck her finger in one pot; the soil felt springy. It looked almost edible—like chocolate cake. Nancy said so.

"She left me a whole cake to eat in the kitchen, do you believe it?" said Gretchen. It wasn't chocolate, though; it was a coffee-cake. And there was fruit, too. "Do you believe it?"

"I hate fruit," Nancy said, even though she didn't; she was distracted. Her eye had been caught by a photograph in a frame on an end table.

"But you don't hate cake, do you? How could anybody?"

"Who's that?" Nancy asked.

"That's her. Mrs. Warren," said Gretchen. "And she looks exactly like it."

"Well, why wouldn't she?—I mean, if it's her."

The photo showed a lady smiling straight out of the picture—not with a full smile. It was the half-smile people wore when they *knew* something. What did she know? The square neck of her yellow sun dress showed the faint pencil line between her breasts.

"She's really nice," said Gretchen. But Nancy had already gone into the next room, actually an enclosed sun porch her parents had used for their bedroom. It was the room Nancy had looked into from outside. The TV was on, laughing. But Nancy wasn't looking at the TV, she was looking at the piano. Nancy had always wanted a piano. Now here one was.

She pressed a note at the bottom of the keyboard, and the whole piano rumbled. She was surprised to feel it in her chest. So even a different kind of *sound* filled the air here now. She played several notes together, using both hands.

"Don't fool around with it, okay?" said Gretchen.

"I'm not fooling around!"

Nancy headed next for the kitchen; she was getting angry. Something made her heart knock and flutter. She began to feel rushed. "When are they coming back?" she asked, but Gretchen didn't hear. Whatever the answer, there wouldn't be enough time to see all there was to see here, the really important, hidden things. Like what the lady in the photo was smiling about.

Of course the kitchen was different, too, and Nancy blinked and blinked, unable to quite believe the transformation. Everything, so immaculate. But it wasn't just the cleanliness. Nancy's own mother went on whirlwind cleaning sprees; afterward, though, things looked merely raw. Now the place was organized. And arranged. There were new cabinets and counters. Plus, a new sink, stove, and refrigerator. They'd kept no remnant of the family who had lived here before them.

"You know something?" Nancy said, but didn't continue. She'd keep it to herself that this was how she had always wanted things to look; the Ouellettes hadn't even put forks and spoons and knives in their separate places in the drawer, though one night, after the supper dishes, Nancy had straightened everything out. She had taken speed at school, an orange heart-shaped tablet; it was one of many days she had taken the drug—but that had been the first time; and it had turned out to be the best. It had made her love everybody and want everything neat, both. And, at the time, it had seemed possible.

The food was all laid out, including thick-skinned oranges and huge black grapes. Gretchen cut herself a flaky wedge of cake, but Nancy had no time for eating. She went back into the front hallway and up the stairs, taking them as she always had before, two at a time.

She went into her brother's room first. There was no bed—in fact, it wasn't a bedroom anymore—there was just a big desk on which sat a dictionary in a tilting book stand, a brass lamp, a notebook. In this room, Nancy's brother had slept in a pink plastic car bed, which he'd wanted so badly when he was ten, but by the time the Ouellettes had finally bought him one, he had outgrown not only the bed itself but also the very idea of it. When Mrs. Ouellette had been pregnant with him, Nancy had shouted into her open mouth, hoping to communicate with the baby. They hadn't done much better since.

She pulled open a drawer of the desk and found more neatness —a stapler, paper clips. She looked at the scissors, so sharp, they frightened her. She put them back in the drawer, shoved as far back as they would go. Then she saw a box of stationery, with her very own address on it. She would take some and write Brent a letter. And he would have to read it if it was written on such nice paper. And he would have to reply. But, no. His letter wouldn't come to her, if he used the return address on this paper—this wasn't her street anymore. The house they lived in now was on a street not as nice. In North, not South Lawrence. It was plain, with tiny rooms. It was what they could afford, said her father. White aluminum siding, black-topped yard. And next door: Puerto Ricans and garbage.

She put the stationery back.

Gretchen had followed Nancy up the stairs and into the room, eating grapes. Nancy asked, "They aren't coming home soon, are they?"

"Ten," said Gretchen. It was nine-thirty or even later now. And as if it had just dawned on her, Gretchen added, "So you'd better hurry up. I mean, like, I guess you could *be* here, but you couldn't be looking around at things like this. You know I'd really get in trouble."

"Where'd they go?"

"To Boston."

"Well, won't they be home later than ten?"

"They said ten, Nance!"

"Okay, okay," said Nancy.

She headed for her old room next where what she had come for was hidden. On the way down the hall she peeked into the room that used to be her grandmother's. The dying smell was gone. She flicked on the light and went in. There was a dust ruffle around the double bed. And four ruffle-edged pillows up against the headboard. Nancy picked at her nails—like picking mica off a rock, coming in layers. Then she went to a bureau and started opening drawers; systematically she opened every one— looking for what? She had no idea, but she did seem to be on an urgent search, her eyes blinking like a camera's shutter. Cataloguing everything. It seemed important that nothing escape.

In that room a new closet had been built. She walked into it grim-lipped. Everything was lined up perfectly. Beautiful flimsy dresses on a rack, nubby sweaters folded on a shelf above, pairs of shoes side by side on the floor. A chest of drawers had been built into the closet. She pulled one drawer open and found sweetly scented underwear. Nancy took a handful and brought it to her nose. One pair of underpants was the color of her grandmother's old flesh. She put them back and took another pair, purple—nothing cheap about that purple, though. They were made of silk, the color of a birthmark. Nancy thought they looked like a pair you saved for special occasions—how could they be missed? When Mrs. Warren finally did go looking for them, she'd never remember when last she had seen them. Nancy stuffed them into her pocket.

"What are you, like, doing?" Gretchen asked, twirling an accusing finger at Nancy's hip. The corner of the lingerie was sticking out of Nancy's pocket, like a cat's tongue.

"I need a clean pair. I need to change." She refused to explain any more, because what she said was true. The underpants she was wearing had gotten wet, because of what she and Mark had been doing in his car before they got here. It wasn't her idea—it was his: such baby stuff, not even going all the way.

"I'm gunna get in trouble," Gretchen wailed, lighting a cigarette, holding her hand around it like there was a wind.

"Gretchen, you are not," said Nancy. It was Nancy who had taught Gretchen how to smoke in the first place, having talked her into walking up to the machine at the filling station to buy a pack one night. Nancy had run out. Gretchen smoked nine cigarettes in a row. Nancy had made her continue until she had gotten it right.

Gretchen went downstairs. Was she going to call her sister? She often resorted to consulting with her or some other adult. Gretchen was such a child, no wonder Nancy couldn't help acting like a parent around her.

"I'll be leaving in about two seconds," Nancy called after her, then crossed the threshold into her old room. The hall light was shining so she could see a lot even without flipping on the switch at the door. Of course everything was different. Now the room was like a magazine picture. The main thing was, a lacy white canopy bed stood right in the middle.

Nancy tiptoed over to the bed—a child was sleeping in it—and looked to see what held up the canopy; it resembled the underside of an umbrella—material stretched across ribs. "Hello," said the little girl, who had opened her eyes and was watching Nancy. Only having pretended to be asleep, she was about four years old, or maybe older, or younger—anyway, she looked old enough to tell her parents what she had seen and heard this evening. She looked tiny, crushable, like a miniature blonde movie star. What foolish people her parents were to leave her alone with strangers! It would never be Nancy who would harm her, but someone might; look how easily Nancy had lost her own child.

"What's your name?" the girl asked Nancy.

"I used to live here," said Nancy, looking at all the dolls and toys lined up and the well-furnished dollhouse—and catching the scent of the awakened girl. Old tears. Soft skin. Sweaty hair brushed smooth. It was a sweet smell, though. Mixed with the odor of candy.

"Mine's Melissa," said the girl.

"This was my room, but it didn't look like this when I lived here," said Nancy. "There were lots of orange roses." She meant on the walls. Her father had done the wallpapering himself. Nancy and her mother had picked the paper out. Orange roses in all the various states of blooming. Now there was pale lavender paint in its place. Had they torn the paper off or just painted over the roses?

"We live here now," Melissa said. "Are you my baby sitter's friend?"

Nancy said nothing; she was headed for the secret door inside the closet that led to the attic crawl space, the entry; the crawl space itself was nothing special, but Nancy had thought it was magical when she was just about Melissa's size.

"You shouldn't smoke, it's bad for you," Melissa continued.

"I'm not smoking, it's Gretchen."

"I smell it."

"That doesn't mean *I'm* smoking."

This time it was Melissa's turn to say nothing; anyway, now Nancy was at the crawl space door. Not a full-sized door, it was only about three-foot square. She could crawl through as she had always done, except that it was nailed shut. She could pry the nails up with a hammer. . . . Once she had moved right into that crawl space. After a fight with her parents. She had moved her most private things in with her. A number of them already were in there. She had torn open the pink fiberglass batting— insulation between floor joists —and hid them inside there. The fiberglass flecks—*real* glass, said her father—got into her skin, made her itch everywhere she touched herself, and when finally she had figured out that that's what was doing it, she had to come out and wash her hands, but still the itching persisted. Just as, years later, when her grandmother was dying, itching had plagued the old woman; Nancy and her mother both had scratched her all over until their fingers were tingly.

"What time is it?" Nancy asked the girl.

"I don't know how to tell time," said Melissa.

Nancy grunted. "Where's a clock?"

"In my mother's room."

Nancy didn't move. She knew the clockface would say time was running out; she should leave, she should have come earlier. She looked at the nailed-shut door again. Behind it she had gone to smoke cigarettes, and once she'd nearly set the place on fire.

Someone was ringing the doorbell. Nancy knew who it was, and Gretchen should know, too, but Nancy heard no stirring from her. The bell rang again. Nancy went out into the hallway. "Let him in, for God's sake," she yelled down the stairs. So Gretchen finally opened the door, and Mark trudged in like a soldier on duty, in search of the enemy, looking left and right dramatically. He was skinny, slightly bowlegged, with hair like a piece of the missing shag rug pasted onto his head, touching his rounded shoulders.

"You haven't got a hammer, have you?" Nancy asked him.

"In my car," he said, so proud of that car, of course he'd have a hammer, he practically lived in that car.

"Could you go out and get it and bring it in?"

"What are you going to do?" Gretchen cringed as Mark pivoted around and went back outside. Turned right around like a zombie under Nancy's control. He didn't even shut the door behind him. Gretchen had to.

Nancy went into the bathroom to put on the underpants. New tile. New fixtures. Nancy felt grubby and dirty. She took off her shoes, muddy. Little waffled pieces of mud fell onto the floor. She took off Brent's jacket with the Executioner patch sewn over the pocket. Underneath she was wearing the birthday sweater Mark had given her—the ugliest gift! It had black and yellow horizontal stripes and made her look like a bee. Mark didn't know beautiful things; how could he? Practical Mark who could fix a flat in five minutes. Mark, who always had a line of black grease under his nails and bit them anyway.

"Nancy," Gretchen called, knocking on the bathroom door, which Nancy had remembered to lock. "Nance!" Gretchen called again while Nancy stripped off her jeans and her own underpants, once a peach color, now grayish from laundries ruined by something navy blue. She put them into the waste basket, and stepped into the clean, purple pair of the lady in the photograph.

"Nancy, you gotta get outa here now. Pleeease?" said

Gretchen, but then the doorbell was ringing again, and Gretchen, whimpering, went away.

Nancy met Mark on the stairs, said thanks, and took the hammer.

"Need help?"

"Nope, no thanks. This won't take long. Find a shopping bag or something, though, will you?"

Mark saluted her, and Nancy went back into the bedroom with the hammer.

Melissa was out of bed. She wore a white nightgown, high-collared, long-sleeved. She was turning the crank on one of her toys, but slowly, habitually. "Are you going to build something?" she asked Nancy.

"I'm just going to get something," Nancy said.

Melissa watched while Nancy pried out the first nail—it made a horrendous creak. She was ruining the paint job, but it wasn't her fault. Why should she let these dolls and other things lie unclaimed? She had remembered the dolls when she was pregnant. Her child—she had envisioned a girl—would need dolls to play with. It was her rightful property, and she could get it if she liked. Try and stop her. There was a teenage girl doll, and a teenage boy, and all their clothes, too—of course. There were also baby dolls, very old dolls, which her father had fixed up for her, mainly straightening out their eyes, because they had rolled backwards into their heads. Those stiff little hands and the hole in the crack in the rear, where water leaked from. . . . Actually, they had been her mother's dolls, but Nancy had loved them just as much.

"Have you ever been back behind here?" Nancy asked Melissa, tapping on the crawl space door.

"I'll ask my mother," said Melissa.

"It's not the kind of thing you ask your mother," Nancy said. "This is a place where you can go and hide and do anything you want, and put anything you want. But you have to watch out about stepping in the wrong places." A foot could go right through the plaster of the unfinished floor, Nancy warned her.

When she finally was able to get into the crawl space, though, she found nothing, not even after stretching a lamp cord across the room for more light. Everything was gone. It was just a cold, dark place that made her sneeze, felt gritty to the touch. And was very, very much smaller than she had remembered it. She came back out.

"*Did* you ever go back in there?" Nancy asked Melissa. "*Did* you find those dolls? There were other things, too."

Melissa took steps back, away from Nancy. "No."

"Well, somebody did."

"I'll ask my mother."

"I'll ask her first."

Then they heard Gretchen groan, and the back door slam, and the front door open.

"My parents are home," announced Melissa and ran downstairs, but Nancy didn't follow. She stood perfectly still in Melissa's bedroom, listening.

Mr. Warren's voice was loud. Came booming out of him. "Company? Got lonely?" he was saying sarcastically to Gretchen. He had seen Mark running across the lawn, he said. Mr. Warren's stomach must have been a drum, which he beat, for the words to come out that way.

Mrs. Warren's voice was a flute. A bird song tweeting, going from branch to branch, trying to think of excuses for Gretchen. "Your brother? On an errand?" Nancy liked the sound. After all, Mrs. Warren was another female; she'd understand. Nancy could talk to her, not only about the crawl space, but about other things, too. Maybe meeting her was meant to be. Nancy believed in coincidences. They happened more often than the average person might ever have suspected.

Gretchen was telling the Warrens that the boy who ran across the lawn wasn't really her friend but the friend of another friend of hers, who was upstairs right this minute. Nancy sighed. *Thanks a lot, Gretchen.* But what else was Gretchen supposed to do? So Nancy would go downstairs now before the Warrens came looking for her. Besides, she wanted the full picture of them, not just their voices.

Melissa was the one to introduce her: "She used to live here, sleep in my room, that was *her* room." At least the little girl understood the significance of the succession.

Mrs. Warren said hello. Gretchen had been right. She looked exactly like the photo. The same hair, same eyes, the half-smile for everyone, even those she disapproved of.

Nancy couldn't have been prepared for Mr. Warren, though. He was just so large. Too big for this house. And with a policeman's moustache. Thick, hiding his mouth almost completely. Maybe he only looked gruff, maybe he wasn't quite so angry as he looked.

Nancy said she had come for the things in the crawl space. "But they aren't up there anymore."

"What things?" said Mr. Warren disdainfully.

But his wife knew. "We have them; we thought you intended to leave them. They're in the basement. You should have called me instead of coming over like this, without our permission."

"You should have called me, that's my stuff, and you knew it."

"I'll get it for you," said Mrs. Warren, chastised. She went down into the cellar, heels clicking evenly on the wooden stairs.

Nancy, Gretchen, Melissa, and Mr. Warren stood in a silent circle. Never has this house been so silent, Nancy thought. They all stood around, as if a moment of silence had been declared. She wanted to scream. Finally, apparently, Mr. Warren couldn't stand it, either, because his voice was booming again, and he was reaching down into his pocket to pay Gretchen, and getting her coat out of the hall closet. She'd worn her fancy one—to Nancy it looked like a skunk.

And did Nancy need a ride home, too? Mr. Warren sighed. Nancy stared at him.

"Home," he repeated.

"Yeah, I know, I know," said Nancy, defeated.

When Mrs. Warren came back upstairs with Nancy's things, in two full grocery bags, Nancy accepted them from her without a word. The heads of the dolls were poking out, looking shabby and unreal. The eyes stared or else had rolled back again. Nancy suddenly felt foolish, then found she was no longer able to look at any of the people in this house. She tried but couldn't raise her eyes, too embarrassed to stay here a minute longer.

"Where are you going, Nance?" asked Gretchen as Nancy's feet took her out the door.

She honestly didn't know where she was going as she walked across the lawn, killing the grass like that, her father had always said. It didn't matter now. She would walk home with her bags; well, maybe she would examine it all under a street light; maybe there was something she could throw away. This load was just too cumbersome for the trek ahead. Maybe she'd throw it all away, or else just keep the diary. Still walking, she fished around in the bags and found it, and it seemed tiny: what could possibly be written in it? There was hardly room for anything, much less something worth remembering. It looked more like a diary for a doll than for a real person. She was heading for a circle of light on the other side of the street when she saw Mark coming out of the shadows. Loyal Mark.

He'd moved his car; it was parked around the corner. "Is that the stuff? Let's see," he said. But Nancy said no.

"Let me carry the frigging stuff, at least!"

Nancy let him do that much. He'd never raised his voice at her before.

"Well, what do you wanna do now?" Mark asked her, quiet again, as they drove away. The motor of the car sounded like it was working hard.

"I don't care."

"You don't wanna go home, do you?"

"God, no!"

They drove along the river, past the mills with their windows all lit up—the buildings appeared to float, like ocean cruisers. They drove up the hill to the park where they had started out this evening. It wasn't far from Nancy's new home, close to the northernmost city line, one of the highest points in the area. The whole city was set out below them, the mills sparkling, the third shift working now. From here, you could see that the mills weren't floating after all; that the city was indeed well situated, at least if there wasn't a major flood. Overhead, yellow and red points of light blinked—not planets or even stars but small planes coming out of Lawrence airport.

It was the same, but different. This had changed, too, in just a couple of hours? Nancy couldn't stop looking around her, as if it might well change again, before her eyes. To their right the old abandoned tennis courts, with broken glass sparkling. To their left the huge blue bulb of a water tank, with LAWRENCE written on it. Farther on beyond that, a white shed of some kind, with graffiti, warning signs. Danger.

Nancy began to rant about what was only peripherally on her mind, keeping the larger thought at bay: People were stupid to have baby sitters, she said. Why didn't they just stay home and take care of their own kids? People treated baby sitters like shit. She remembered how she always fell asleep, and then the people had to wake her, and always seemed to resent it, shaking her shoulder only just enough, like they hated to touch her. Then the man would be drunk, and the wife would try to get him upstairs and Nancy would see him anyway. He'd wave like he was fingering a flute. . . . Then Nancy thought of her own lost child again—and the special sadness, like nothing else. A lost opportunity. A whole world of potential. Well, there was something sweet about that, too. Unspoiled. Nancy hadn't had a chance to wreck it.

Suddenly she wanted to see it all closer, the park, that is. "Let's take a walk."

Rocks and clods of grass made their footing unsteady. They walked to the precipice, holding hands, dogs barking behind them. Nancy saw one; he was coming after them, growling, but his tail was wagging, a feathery tail, like a flag raised over his head, waving at them. A hopeless North Lawrence dog, pretending to be so brave, yet unwittingly showing a sign of surrender.

Mark squeezed Nancy's hand harder. She felt the splinter in her finger again—she'd forgotten about it. But she didn't pull her hand back. She knew about pain. She also knew Mark was feeling more affection for her than she was for him. She could feel it in his hand, and anyway she just knew him well enough by now. His palm was damp, but warm. Like something uncooked, that needed to be covered. Like an open part of the body.

She wanted a cigarette, but he wanted to kiss. She didn't want to kiss; she wanted something more real. But Mark was the one who seemed to want to wait. What was he afraid of? "My mother practically gives me kisses like that, can't you be a man with me?"

Mark was saying he loved her and that he had never thought anybody would love him, because of his face. "I don't care about that," said Nancy, and she meant it. She kissed the holes and smelled the cream. And it didn't seem to matter. He was a good person, just a good person.

Was she protected? Was she taking The Pill or something? Because if she wasn't he had something, the best, very expensive. "I don't need anything," said Nancy. "I don't," she insisted. And she wasn't exactly lying; anyway, this time, she wouldn't try to force anybody into anything and get herself all upset and lose it again.

They lay down on the cold earth, and she held on tight, gripping with her thighs. Unlike Brent, whose way with sex was rough and insistent, Mark wanted Nancy to feel something, too. That's what he wanted to be sure of and he wasn't. Did she feel the same thing he did? Did she want the same thing he did? But she couldn't reply.

When it was over, they didn't go back to the car right away. Nancy was still putting the purple underpants back on anyway. *Would* they ever be missed by Mrs. Warren? Maybe they would be, but the woman could prove nothing. Nancy smiled, and, contented for the moment, zipped up her jeans, as if she were sealing something inside her. Then she leaned into Mark and a soft smile came to her lips. They were surrounded by trees and she could really see for the very first time how they were growing up out of the earth. How it was only their roots attached to the earth, while the rest reached up to the sky, purplish-black, darker where the stars could be seen after all, light almost lavender down toward the horizon.

# The Disappearance

"You can drive the devil out of your garden, but you
will find him again in the garden of your son."
—Pestalozzi

T HE GLARE OF THE WET, white sheets as Rosario untwisted
them, and of his wife's enormous underpants, also white,
also twisted, reminded him, as he pinned the laundry to the
clothesline outside his back door, of "Snow-bound" . . . "by John
Greenleaf Whittier." He'd memorized a portion of the poem in
tenth grade, and he'd recited it, wearing his itchy woolen pants
and standing in front of the classroom. He'd done it all right,
too—the teacher, with her apple breasts, had praised him; but
Rosie, as he had been called since he was a boy, had to leave
school shortly afterwards and go to work as a gardener on one
of the estates in the rich town next door to the cramped, unkempt
little city where he'd lived all his life and where his father had
gotten into so much trouble down at one of the mills.

Now, this father's son was a man of seventy with silver locks
of oily hair, almost like rows of sardines, and fierce black eyes
set in a permanent squint from his years spent outdoors. And
he was recently retired. That was why he had no more excuses
to get out of hanging the laundry. His wife Ignatia was too

arthritic to do the job herself. Lena, Ignatia's sister, had been doing it for them all summer, but she was sickly now, too, or so she claimed. A widow who lived alone in a large house three blocks away, Lena clung so to Ignatia, they were like two sides of a peach. Earlier this week Rosie even had to take Lena to the doctor's office. Like *she* was his wife! Lena complained that she felt dizzy and had difficulty drawing breath. But as Rosie had walked with her toward Dr. Fettinger's door, she'd confessed to him that she sometimes *held* her breath. Rosie had stopped short, stared at her lifting her glasses to dab at her eyes and heavily powdered nose with a balled-up kleenex, and said to her, "*Breathe*," bending his knees on his own intake. "Take a breath of air, for Chrissakes! What else have you got to do?" Lena also had complaints the doctor could not name. But Rosie could. "It's nerves," he told a neighbor, Mr. Pasquerelli. Other people on the block called Mr. Pasquerelli "The F.B.I." He hung around the street corner, wearing dark glasses, watching out for "things—funny business . . . kids—you know, the jerks." Rosie told Mr. Pasquerelli that Lena should take a shot now and then, the way he himself did. "That'd fix her right up." Then he paused. Something about the waiting room had upset him, he told Mr. Pasquerelli's dark glasses, the cracked white lips waiting under them: "There were all *old* people in there. Nobody young. Don't kids get sick anymore or what?"

Inside their ground-floor apartment, Rosie's and Ignatia's grandson Vin, who used to let himself be called "Vinnie" until just this school year, stood by the glossy kitchen table. His black eyelashes were closely bunched, he was tall for fourteen, and his muscles were long and lean, so mostly hidden. "How'd you get here?" Ignatia asked him, shuffling over to the table from the stove. She wore men's bedroom slippers with holes cut out for her bunions. "You hitchhike? You're going to get murdered one of these days. Who picked you up? A man or a woman? The women are worse than the men sometimes. You have to be careful, every minute of your life."

The boy told his grandmother that he was very careful and that he had ridden his bike.

"Your hair looks good," she said, reaching up to smooth it.

"Before you were born, boys wanted to look like girls. Like your Uncle Patsy. And don't think Luca didn't cut his hair for him but good one time." Luca, their landlord, an old friend of Rosie's father, was a retired tailor who lived upstairs and always wore a white shirt and dark tie knotted up close to his throat. He was slightly bent now, but still moved quickly, like a young person with an injury.

"Rosie held Patsy down right out there in the garden while Luca did the cutting," Ignatia said. "You don't believe me?"

"I believe you, Gram," Vin said.

"Our own son. I did nothing to stop it. Now I'm sorry. Well, sit, siddown," Ignatia said, sitting heavily herself, as if to show how it was done. "Sit, sit, have a cup of coffee."

"Just tell me why you wanted me to come over," Vin said.

"I'm going to ask you a favor."

"I know, Gram. Just tell me what it is."

"Did that storm wake you up last night?" Ignatia pressed a clutched fist to the middle of her chest. "I had the sheet pulled up over my head just like Lena and I used to do when we were kids. St. Christopher here, St. Michael there." She touched the top of each of her breasts, doughy cushions. "And the rosary beads around my hand!" She laughed girlishly, then gathered together the two parts of her housecoat, its color the green of cheap ice cream, the print worn to illegibility. She adjusted the safety pins that had replaced its lost buttons, holding them in her mouth at intervals, like a mother doing a diaper; then pushed a plate of almond cookies at him. He took one, but just held it in his hand, didn't bite down. She herself was never much on sweets, either, she said. The real food—the meat!—that was the important thing. She poured coffee into her cup from a thermos, then she poured it from the cup into the saucer and lapped it up from there, lifting it to her mouth with both hands.

"I didn't sleep a wink the night *before* the storm, either," she said. She had felt the pains in her heart again. And then the palpitations. "But as long as I can talk about it, I'm all right. Right?"

"Right," said Vin, but she could see he'd grown impatient. He'd come all the way from the next town. He was a good boy to obey her.

Finally she told him what he was to do: buy her a money

order that she would give to Patsy, so he could pay his rent. She gave Vin cash: $400 in twenty-dollar bills. He was to bring the money order back to her tomorrow and then she'd mail it to Patsy in Boston for a surprise.

"He wasn't dishonest—that's why he's a failure," Ignatia said. "He could have made a lot of money at one time, you know."

As Vin started to leave, Ignatia pressed an extra twenty into the hand of his that was in his jeans pocket.

"No, Gram, I can't take that," he said, finally eating the cookie he still held, needing his other hand free to try resisting her.

"Take."

"I don't want to."

"But I want."

"Just say me a prayer or something."

Ignatia hugged him hard just as Rosie came in from the garden, tomatoes, not quite ripe, rolling around in the plastic laundry basket. "I wanted to pick them before the frost got them," he said, looking suspiciously from Ignatia to Vin and back. It was a little unusual for the boy to show up here like this after school. What would Rosie think when the boy showed up here again tomorrow?

"You put them in a paper bag to ripen," Ignatia said. "Did you know that, Vinnie?"

"Yes, Gram."

"How does a boy like you know a thing like that?" One more time she reached up to touch his closely shorn head.

Rosie bent down to pinch suckers from the tomato vines while Vin retrieved his bike from the tool shed. Rosie had made him stash it in there, not just lock it. So many Slippery Sam's walking the streets of Lawrence nowadays. "Puerto Ricans!" Near the peeling, warped-boarded shed, roses, red and white, still bloomed, heavy heads touching the ground, the sleepy scent wafting up. Ladies in church wore roses like that on their hats: artificial. At least they used to: Rosie hadn't been to church in years. How many real roses had he pruned, sprayed, been stuck by?

"You have a girlfriend yet?" Rosie lifted his white-stubbled chin to ask Vin his dead-serious question. "Or are you going to be a fruit like your Uncle Patsy? Your brother has a beautiful girlfriend. Doesn't she have a younger sister for you?" Rosie scratched his behind, smiling to himself, thinking about Peter's girlfriend. "She's a real girl."

Vin agreed. Sometimes he spied on Peter and Maggie. Today, after school, on his way over here, he'd watched them whacking golfballs on her front lawn. Vin had crouched down behind some bushes, watching until they went into the house by the side door: an immense house. It was made of honey-colored stone and the lawn was like green snow, that perfect. A gardener had been moving along the edge of it, a pair of clippers in his hand. Then he spotted Vin, who ran to his bike, surprised that the man could be so angry, acting as if it were his own property.

"What did you want to come over here for today?" Rosie asked Vin. He gestured toward the kitchen, his fingers stained yellow by the tomato plants.

"A favor," Vin said simply.

"Something about Patsy, am I right?"

"A favor, that's all."

Rosie nodded grimly at the kitchen window. "I don't know what happened to that one in there," he said, catching a glimpse of Ignatia fuming at him through the curtains. "She let herself go, watching those stories, stuffing herself with candy. She used to be like this, you know." Rosie blew a breath across his palm. "See where I got the calluses?" He pointed. "On either side of the wedding band. See that? Nowhere else. See? Feel them. *Feel.*" Vin touched his grandfather's hand.

Ignatia went into her bedroom and put on a wide dress. She rouged her face, making two red circles, swiped her eyelids with a blue dust, and hung a dangling ornament from each ear. Then she forced her arms through the sleeves of an old black cloth coat. Rosie softly swore when he saw her. This was her going-out look. He'd forgotten that today he took her food shopping. He trudged through the garden to back the car out of the garage. The furry white sun was gone. Another storm coming? Rosie swore under his breath again. He'd let the clothes stay on the line, anyway. Maybe it would pass over.

While Rosie waited for Ignatia, he watched a downtown

smoke stack puffing purple, and a sullen orange cat saunter across the street. It was a tom just like the one his mother had chased with a broom after she'd found it on her bed, eating the drying spaghetti. A stranger's cat, no less; that had upset her the most. She and Rosie were living with her sister Rocchina by then. This was shortly after Rosie's father's disappearance, during the strike of '31. Twenty-three thousand had walked out of the mills, but Saverio Rosario had to be one of the few arrested on the picket line. His crime? Assaulting a policeman for arresting another picketer, who had called the officer "a cucumber," in dialect. Not such a terrible insult, in any language. Even if he'd said something worse, the policeman shouldn't have been so rough with him.

The papers said that all the arrested men's claims of citizenship would be investigated. Saverio's face burned with anger under his cap at that one; or so Rosie imagined. After the day of his arrest, neither Rosie nor his mother ever saw Rosie's father again. Where had he gone? The police claimed Saverio escaped. The Reds from Harvard cried: "Murder!" saying he'd been beaten to death in his cell, the body disposed of. But neither the police nor the Reds had ever produced a body, dead or living. Still, Rosie's mother had cried into the bloodied clothes that a member of the Young Communists had brought her. What did Rosie think? Even after all these years, he wasn't sure, though he'd never much liked policemen—never mind that his own daughter had married one: Vin's and Peter's father. Rosie wasn't too crazy for Communists, either, but if he didn't believe what they had said, if his father had escaped after all, and had never called for Rosie and his mother, that meant he had deserted them.

"Nice!" Ignatia said on her way down the back-yard path to the car. She was admiring the boughs of roses falling against the shed, though she couldn't help but point out that she and Rosie didn't own them. Or the house.

"You were *afraid* to buy a house," she said to begin their old argument. "We could have had this house, upstairs *and* down."

"I paid for this house, every month," Rosie said quietly.

"You could have paid for your own house," she said. "But no: 'What if the roof caves in?' That's what you always said."

"Do you have any idea how much a new roof costs?"

"Oh, you're so smart," she said.

"Well, do you?"

She flung her hand to signal that she had given up on him again.

"Well, you're traveling light, look at it that way," Rosie said.

"Traveling light? Honey. Where am I traveling *to*?"

In the grocery store Rosie walked broodingly behind her as she pushed the cart along, using it as a kind of walker, then made leaps away from it for the food, once embracing a whole armload of tomato cans before dumping them in. Sometimes, Rosie noticed, she forgot her "arthuritis" completely, for example, when she pinched and prodded a bag of seeded rolls to see how fresh they felt through the plastic. "Corn on the cob should have handles on *both* ends," she told herself and others at the vegetable bins. She criticizes God himself, thought Rosie, who, as usual, just followed along with his hands knotted behind his back, knowing from long years of experience that if he even picked so much as a roll of toilet paper, there'd be something wrong with it; she'd have to put it back and choose another. Then, wouldn't you know it, today, in the frozen foods aisle, a man about Patsy's age, forty-five this month, began to glare accusingly at Rosie while Ignatia stood on her toes to reach across the frosty bins to claim the exact canister of bread crumbs she wanted.

"What's your problem, pal?" Rosie asked the kinky-haired man. The glasses he wore were round black circles like those drawn on posters to deface them.

"She's having trouble. You could help her."

"Says who?"

"I say. I see her struggling."

"Yeah. She struggles like a snake."

The man glared at Rosie again through the portholes of his glasses.

"You think she needs so much help," said Rosie, "you help her. See what happens."

"Oh, thank you, no thank you," said Ignatia to the man, who shrugged and moved along, still glaring at Rosie over his shoulder.

"He's smoking reefers, that guy," said Rosie.

At the checkout counter he wearily took out his wallet to pay while Ignatia supervised the boy in his apron who loaded the food into bags. She waited until they were wheeling the cart out to the parking lot before she said: "He was right, you know."

"Who?"

"The one that told you to help me. You could, you know."

"That guy should be in a straightjacket somewheres."

"You should be as crazy as he is. He looks like a smart boy."

"Living with you, I'm crazier."

"Lena! She's the only one who understands me."

"Go! Live with Lena. Who's stopping you?"

"We'll both be living with her soon enough, when Luca goes."

"I'd rather chew grape seeds with the bums down under the bridge."

"You might be. Don't laugh."

Rosie mumbled something else, then drove recklessly up and over a curb on his way out of the parking lot. "Jesus, Mary, and Joseph," Ignatia said as they headed for the highway ramp. The car wheezed and lurched up the incline, and then, just as they were about to join the traffic barreling up behind them, lost power. Rosie pressed the pedal to the floor, but they still crept dangerously along the edge of the highway. When another driver trying to get into the flow of cars finally got the chance to screech past them, swearing out the window at Rosie, shaking his index finger at him, Rosie drew his elbow across his face, as if ready to strike anyone who could be as impatient as that. Couldn't he see a man in trouble? "Jesus Christ!" Rosie said as he steered into the breakdown lane.

They sat. "My Mother, My Confidence, My Mother, My Confidence," Ignatia droned. Then Rosie saw in the rear-view mirror a little pickup truck had pulled over behind them. A woman in jeans and boots hopped out and walked purposefully to Ignatia's side of the car.

"Have you got far to go?" the young woman asked; she looked rugged and healthy and unafraid of anything; her lips were thin, her eyes clear.

"God bless you!" Ignatia said. "One exit. My husband was showing off. He doesn't have any business driving on here."

"I can run you home."

"Could you, honey?"

"No problem."

"My husband'll ride in the truck part," Ignatia offered for Rosie.

"I think we could all fit up front, if we squeeze," the woman said.

"Good-bye," said Rosie.

"You really want to stay here?" the woman asked.

"Good-bye, I told you."

"I'll call Jimmy," Ignatia said. "Our son-in-law, a policeman," she proudly explained, struggling to get herself and her big black oily bird of a pocketbook out of the car. "Jimmy would say not to take a ride with anybody, but would a bad person stop and be so nice?"

When the door had latched shut behind her, and the truck was a speck disappearing down the highway, Rosie closed his eyes. *Peace.* If he had to walk home, so what? It'd do him good. Since he'd retired, he'd put on some weight, though his twenty-year-old pants and cardigan had never fit him well. Besides, the storm clouds were moving away, ragged and swift; through the breaks he could see blue.

"The sun, a snowblown traveler, sank/From sight beneath the smothering bank...." He'd recited "Snow-bound" for his father. Habitually, when he was in trouble, Rosie thought of him and his neat black moustache, trim waist and thighs, strong arms that reached for the lunch pail Rosie would run down to the mill to deliver. The man was just thirty-four years old when Rosie saw him last; that was in the fall of '31, when they sat together at the kitchen table and drank coffee while Rosie read him the strike news in the paper, translating it into Italian as he went along. Saverio had come in late and eaten the fried dough, sprinkled with sugar, that they had saved him from supper. After that he'd settled into his stuffed armchair in the living room, the antimacassar crocheted by Rosie's mother in place behind his head, plastered to the edge of the upholstery by his hair oil. Rosie was fifteen. When he was four or five, he'd hidden behind that same chair, counting on his fingers to come up with the right answer when his father drilled him in his sums. Though the man knew few English words, he knew English numbers well enough: that was money. The big armchair was also the place where Rosie's father sat to write letters for people—in Italian; they came to the house and told him what they wanted to say; he wrote in his small straight hand on whatever scraps of paper they had brought with them.

After the disappearance, however, everything changed. Rosie got old, fast—especially since he'd had to leave school. One minute, he was a boy full of the devil, sitting in the back of the class, whittling away at a pencil; the next, he had a shovel in his hand, standing in someone else's mud. He was a gray-haired boy in no time. And he still hadn't stopped daydreaming that his father had become rich and would return to rescue him. His night dreams included him, too—in the rare times when he dreamt. He had trouble sleeping. To make it worse, Ignatia snored. He could hear the racket—like a door opening and slamming shut, over and over—even from the next room where his bed was.

And where would he sleep at Lena's? She lived in the big cedar-shingled house across the street from the German Old Folks Home. Alfred had done well. A saint, to hear Lena tell it. He had risen to a supervisor role in the Bradford Silk Underwear Mills, and wasn't it just his dumb good luck to be gone by the time the company went under? When he died in his forties, Alfred left Lena with a fat insurance payoff. His early death may have been a good thing in disguise for Lena; she seemed happier without him. And she couldn't claim to be lonely. Not only a widow, she'd had no children—she was all sealed up: even her hair, in tight bronzed curls, looked impenetrable, like rows of spray-painted seashell macaroni—but, except in the dead of night, Lena's constant companion was her sister Ignatia.

And if he and Ignatia moved in with her? No, something would have to prevent that. But if it did happen, would he have to go back to sharing a bedroom with Ignatia? Or would Lena give them each their own room? Or would the two sisters share a room, so they could whisper in the dark? Whatever the arrangement, he'd be humiliated. He'd be a guest, everyone would know his business. This would be the slowest death. And if Ignatia were to die? Would he have to spend the rest of his days in the same house with Lena? That would be the worst possibility of all. Or would she kick him out? Well, why give her a chance to? He could avoid all that by never agreeing to live there in the first place.

After a while, Rosie got out of the car and looked under the hood. A distributor wire was disconnected. So that was the trouble. He reconnected it and got the car to start. I could just keep on driving, he thought. But he didn't. He merely drove cautiously home. For one thing, he had to urinate badly. The old man's disease. Ignatia was in the garden cutting roses when he pulled up outside the gate.

"I called Jimmy. They're sending somebody to go find you, for nothing, I guess," she said. "And don't forget the packages. We'll have garbage in five minutes more."

He watched her with narrowed eyes from the bathroom window, unseen. She'd taken off her shoes and put her slippers back on, though she still wore her black coat. She'd brought her wooden cane out to the garden to lean on; she had a pair of red-handled scissors in her other hand, and she'd laid a piece of newspaper on the grass. As she snipped the roses, she dropped them onto the paper. Then she stopped, as if to listen hard to something. "Rosie!" she called. Rosie glowered, saying nothing, still spying on her. Couldn't a man have a little peace, even in the bathroom? Where would his dignity go in Lena's house? She only had one bathroom, right next to her bedroom. Ignatia continued to call him. She was swearing at him, too. When he was finished, he went to see what her hollering was all about.

He reached the threshold of the back door in time to see her fall. As if she'd waited for him, so that he might see the spectacle: she rolled, like a great black boulder, or two men fighting, rolling over one another on the ground. Rosie picked up the scissors first. Wasn't that what any sensible man would do? The rose heads were strewn everywhere as if a flower girl had done it.

She wouldn't let him help her up. She just lay on the ground, yelling at him in her mother's language. She was wishing to God that her father had never left the *fattoria*, meaning "farm," but Rosie reminded her that *fattoria* also meant "factory"—on this side of the world it did.

"I wouldn't have fallen if you'd come to help me when I called you the first time," she said with her cheek to the ground.

"Damn roses," he mumbled. "I had to go to the bathroom. Is that a crime?" He gathered the roses up on the newspaper. A headline caught his eye, something about an ex-priest. He carried the roses into the house and put them on the kitchen table, then returned to the garden.

"I went to work—I should have gone to school." She was still on the ground, digging her elbows into the grass. "Left sole, left shoe, right sole, right shoe—you think it was easy? Everybody used to walk to work, all those feet wearing down shoes. Good for business. Nobody walks anywhere anymore. Oooh, but I feel like somebody just walked all over me."

Rosie put his hands underneath her moist armpits, and pulled her to her feet. He handed her the cane. "I was getting roses to put by the statue. His flower. The Sacred Heart," she said.

"Good thing this didn't happen on the stairs," said Rosie. "See? You're lucky we don't live in a whole big house."

"I was getting roses for Him and look what happens," she said, and gave her cane a little shake, pointing it up toward Heaven.

"Well, the roses'll cheer you up," he said when she finally got her bearings and they were standing in the garden together.

When Vin heard that evening of his grandmother's fall, he lay across his bed and started writing his poem called "Maggie." His grandmother was like a mountain to him, with one of those rock-slide warnings at the bottom. You looked up and saw rocks about to topple, but you couldn't believe that they ever would. His mother Lobelia talked about how old her mother Ignatia looked, but to Vin she was like a mountain in that, too—not aging except in ways you wouldn't notice. *Fourteen years old.* Was that young? He thought so, but every time he saw himself in the mirror, he was shocked. The top of his head was edging up toward the top of the mirror. He could make his chest look broad, especially if he held his breath. His father and brother had noticed his growth. So now they had started testing him, holding him down on his bed and fighting with him, both of them together, to toughen him up, they said.

Vin wrote another line of his poem: "Maggie, your eyes are like two blue daisies...," then crossed out the word "two." How many eyes did anybody ever have, unless they were a cyclops or something, dodo bird.

Bored by the poem, he began to think about the money his grandmother had given him for Patsy's money order. Maybe he could say the money was lost, or stolen. Then he could spend it. But could he do that to his Uncle Patsy? The turd. As his grandfather said, "Lawyers are supposed to make a lot of money, right? Not Patsy. Noooo. He's too smart for that. He's just like my father," Rosie said. "Couldn't leave well enough alone. Had the Devil in him. Had to meddle. Had to tell people what he thought. Now Patsy's going around doing the same: defending bums. His own people aren't good enough for him."

Peter came into the room after Vin had written a few more lines to Maggie. "What's that? What is it?" He grabbed the piece of notebook paper out of Vin's hand. Vin leapt and landed on his brother's back and pounded him with his fists; Vin tore the paper into bits in order to get it away from him. "All right, God, you're a wild man," said Peter, who, lucky for Vin, had not been able to see that his own girlfriend's name was written on it.

The next day at school, Vin showed Maggie the roll of bills. "Yeah? So?" She was dressed entirely in pink, including scuffless pink leather aerobic shoes. Vin's eyes searched for a speck of dirt. How did she keep so clean? She pretended to yawn. "So what?" Of course, she'd be unimpressed with money, but she did seem interested in where a kid like him might have gotten it. Peter was even more interested. His eyes grew wide. "Where'd you get that? You stole it!" He snatched at the money.

"I did not."

"Got any more? Gimme that."

Peter grabbed the money out of his hand—easily, because Vin would not risk tearing that. Peter slid it into his jeans pocket, and he and Maggie strolled down the corridor. If Peter spent it, if he didn't give it back, that *was* stealing. If Peter told his parents what Vin had brought to school, Vin would tell the truth, and his grandmother would back him up. Unless she died. Unless she was already dead, this morning. Why didn't all old people just die? Why didn't everybody—just get it over with and die?

After school, Vin again rode his bike to see Ignatia and told her what Peter had done. "You'll get it back from him, honey," she said, lying on her bed; the dark pigment around her eyes looked like a burglar's mask. She said she was sore all over. She really didn't care about anything right now except getting better. She would take care of it later. "Tell Peter to come see me in a couple of days. I'll tell him what I think about things. I'll give him one of these. You know?" She made a motion, half karate chop, half a spank for a baby's bottom. "Have an apple or a banana on the way out. On the kitchen table in the nice big bowl. Ahhh, I used to feed the birds. They used to see me coming. I'd walk home from work along Union Street, and they'd flock all around me, like I was St. Francis or something. Now I feed birds like you."

Rosie didn't speak to Vin as he left by way of the garden. The two of them—Vin and Ignatia—were in cahoots, doing something for Patsy, and Rosie would find out sooner or later what it was. Rosie had phoned Patsy last night to tell him about his mother's fall, and to say that a call from him would cheer her up. But he hadn't been able to get through to Patsy. Not even after midnight. At six, this morning, Rosie had been awake, but didn't think of Patsy until seven. And by then there was no answer once again. Patsy, gone to work early. Or else he hadn't spent any time at all in his apartment last night.

Luca, his landlord, his father's old friend, hadn't been at home upstairs last night, for certain. Doctor's orders. Yesterday he'd been told that he wasn't to spend the night alone anymore, so he had stayed with his son Dennis and daughter-in-law in West Boxford. He wasn't allowed to drive, either, but shortly after Vin pedalled away, along came Luca driving without permission, like a teenager. He had things to attend to in the apartment, he told Rosie in his accented English. "There's something in there for you, too, you'll see. You'll get it. You wait." And the way he said it, Rosie could guess that meant he'd have to wait until after Luca was dead.

Luca took a few wobbly steps to the garden border and pinched off a yellow coreopsis head. He slipped the short stem into the breast pocket of his jacket; the flower poked out. He broke off another one and handed it to Rosie, who could never help but get annoyed whenever Luca acted like he owned the place, even if he was the landlord. Luca had heard about Ignatia's fall. He wanted to see her. Together he and Rosie walked inside. Luca weaved; Rosie took hold of his elbow. "I'm all right," the old man said, brushing him away.

The house smelled of burned food. Rosie had ruined some fried peppers and onions he'd tried to make for lunch, though he'd done all right with breakfast. The only thing he'd done wrong was to spill the coffee trying to pour it into the thermos. He wore a bandage on his forearm where the liquid had scalded him. He had affixed a square of gauze and tape with the help of Lena, who'd been there around mid-morning. Her dizziness had miraculously disappeared, she had said as she'd fussed over Ignatia and puttered in the kitchen.

When Luca walked into Ignatia's room, she was sitting up, cleaning the statue of the Sacred Heart, polishing it with a cotton dish towel. She was sorry now for what she had said against God in the garden.

As she and Luca chatted, Rosie began to wonder what Luca had for him upstairs. Could it be money? Wouldn't it have to be? What if it was the deed to the whole house? Luca's children would fight it, but Rosie would win the case. He'd get Patsy to help him. Then Rosie scolded himself; Luca was not going to leave him his property; that was a ridiculous thought. If anybody'd looked inside his head while that was passing through it, they'd have said he was nuttier than Patsy.

"One thing about being sick, everybody comes see you," Luca laughed.

"Lobelia's been here, and Vinnie. Peter's busy with his girlfriend. And Patsy, he's so busy, too," said Ignatia.

Rosie watched Luca closely. Why was he going to make him wait until after he was dead to get whatever he was going to give him? Driving around in his condition, Luca'd probably be dead before the day was out. And take two or three people with him. But what are you gonna do? After Luca went creakily up the stairs to his apartment, Rosie phoned Dennis to tell him his father was here. The sooner Luca died, the sooner he'd get his gift, if it was a gift; but also the sooner he and Ignatia would be packing off to Lena's.

"My wife thought somebody *stole* the car," Dennis told Rosie on the phone from his office. "Then she figured it out. She's on her way."

Later, Rosie saw the old man walking to his daughter-in-law's car with his hands out, like someone in pitch darkness feeling for walls.

A few weeks after that, Rosie dressed in his one good suit to attend Luca's wake. Outside it was a bright fall day, leaves crackled underfoot; inside the funeral home, it was spring: wreaths and flowers made the whole place stink, thought Rosie, who recognized many of his own old acquaintances among the throng, including his neighbor Pasquerelli.

Rosie knelt solemnly at the casket. Luca's waxen face was rouged, wearing lipstick, too. Behind Rosie, people talked loudly, reminiscing. "Fabrizio Pitocchelli's bank. Remember how it went bankrupt? Five hundred thousand dollars. That's the Depression. Today, a football player couldn't buy his underwear with that...." "Neapolitans didn't have much money in that bank—they ate their money...." "LoPiano ate his and everybody else's after he went to New Jersey with those stolen money orders...." They laughed.

*Eighty-nine years old*. That was Luca's age. Rosie's father would be that age, too, if he had lived. If he still did live somewhere today. Rosie moved to the receiving line to pay his respects to Luca's family.

"How's Ignatia?" Dennis asked Rosie as they shook hands. He had a tan. He was one of those fifty-year-olds who still dressed like a kid.

"She was sorry she couldn't be here herself to tell you how bad she feels," Rosie said, though, at home, Ignatia, hearing the news of Luca's death, had been not sad but elated. Now they really could go live with Lena. They might have gone sooner, but it was only polite to wait until the old man died, considering his kindnesses to them over all these years. He would never have gotten new tenants as good as they were, not in a million years. Of course Dennis and the others would have had him sell the building long ago, but Luca wouldn't stand for that. Now all Ignatia and Rosie had to do was wait for Lena's formal invitation.

The wake was followed by a huge funeral the next day. Then, after the burial, a party back at the house of Luca's daughter, in Methuen. At the buffet table, where Rosie had gone to hide from Mr. Pasquerelli, he found himself standing right next to Dennis again.

"Doesn't that guy have a home?" Rosie asked Dennis of Pasquerelli.

"He used to deliver mail to my father's shop," Dennis said.

Rosie nodded, remembering that Pasquerelli's first career, as a postal worker, reading everybody's envelopes and postcard messages, had prepared him for his second career as a neighborhood spy. Rosie was about to make this observation to Dennis, but when he turned to him Dennis said, solemnly as a judge, "Rosie, I know you're probably concerned about what we're going to do with the house. I want you know that we'd like you to take all the time you need to get resettled. I'm going to have some people come over and look at the property, but they're not to disturb you. Nothing's going to happen quickly. You take all the time in the world. You'll hear me cleaning things out upstairs. Don't worry. I think there's something up there for you, as a matter of fact."

Rosie ate a black olive. He knew these words must be considered one more kindness of the Luca family, and he knew he should thank Dennis, but he could bring himself to say nothing. He nodded and watched Dennis filling his plate with cole slaw, and Pasquerelli drifting toward him.

"Where've you been?" Pasquerelli asked. "I haven't seen you around."

"You know us gardeners. We're like the bears. We hibernate. In the spring, you'll see us again."

"Ignatia. How's she doing?"

"She still got complaints. Arthuritis, her heart . . ."

"Woman trouble?"

"Me? I'm too old for that."

"You know what I mean. Ignatia."

"I don't know if she's got any or not. I haven't checked lately."

"That's what it always is with them, don't you think?"

"Myself, I don't speak for women," said Rosie.

When Rosie returned home, Ignatia said, "What happened? What did people say?" He told her what Dennis had told him. "Well, Ro, Lena has said she'd have us come live with her. It's all set. All we have to do is say the word."

The first snow came early that year, just a few weeks after the funeral, while Dennis was cleaning out his father's apartment. Rosie could hear him overhead and see the white flakes falling past the blackness of the tree branches spread out across his downstairs window. The snow was falling wet and fast, sticking as if each piece were carrying a bit of glue. The chatter of the television was coming from Ignatia's room. Rosie had convinced her to stay here, to put off moving to Lena's, at least until they had received the gift promised, whatever it was, from Luca. "You never know," Rosie said. "Oh, yes you do," said Ignatia, but she agreed to wait.

Dennis came to the door as he was leaving, with a bundle of letters.

"Come in, come in," Rosie said.

"No, I gotta get home, but these are for you. Your name. From my father."

The dates of the postmarks began 1931, '32, '33 . . . The handwriting that had written Luca's name and address looked familiar; then Rosie saw the return address: a place in Italy and the name and first initial, S. Rosario.

Rosie sat and read of his father's life, gripped by a fear that he wouldn't get to the end of the letters. His heart pounded irregularly against the wall of his chest. So! he kept saying to himself as he read the faded ink written in his father's patchwork Italian. So! The Reds had *paid* Saverio to disappear, to go back to Italy. At a time when men were waiting in line for a slice of bread and salt pork, they had enticed him with money, saying that, with him gone, they could more easily claim, as they had done, that the police had murdered him in his cell and hidden the body. Produce the body of Saverio Rosario, the Reds would demand of the police; and of course they wouldn't be able to. The deal was that they would send Rosie and his mother back to Italy soon after, and this was what Rosie's father had intended all along. And so he fled.

Rosie's mother had not followed that plan, however. She was paralyzed, with fear. She wouldn't budge; she'd just gotten here to America, she said, though it had already been nearly seventeen years. Rocchina, her sister, who had just then lost her husband in a mill fire, was begging her to stay; she would die of loneliness, otherwise. And so they did stay. And Saverio had written Luca all these letters to urge him to get Rosie's mother to change her mind, to consider his own state of loneliness. Apparently, he had been writing her letters, too, but she hadn't answered. And Saverio couldn't return to America because of the new immigration laws.

After he finished reading the letters, Rosie just stared out the window; for a long time, he just watched the crazy people driving by in the slippery snow. Then Ignatia was calling him from her bedroom. "Ro, Vinnie's here. I can see him coming through the gate, wheeling his bike."

"Don't you listen to weather reports?" Rosie asked him at the door.

"Yeah, I listen, but I don't always believe them."

"Come in, come in."

Vin knocked the snow off his shoes and shed his clothes for warm ones of Rosie's.

"Where were you going on your bike on a day like today?"

"Out."

"Out where."

"Away."

"Running away?"

Vin said nothing, just covered his face with the towel he was using to dry his hair.

"I thought so. I saw that look. Come on, come on now, get warm. Go sit on the radiator."

Vin obeyed while Rosie fixed him some coffee and two large fried-egg sandwiches.

"Where's the bike?"

"Out there."

"Not in the shed?"

"I didn't even lock it," Vin shrugged.

"Why not?"

"Who's going to steal a bike in this weather?"

"Thieves'll steal anytime."

Rosie went out to attend to the bike. He found it leaning up against the house. He wheeled it toward the snow-topped shed. It had been a while since he'd walked along with a bike at his side. The movement brought with it a feeling of freedom he used to know. Or maybe he'd only dreamed of such a feeling, of being free to go anywhere, to make himself at home anywhere in the world.

Inside the house, Ignatia called to Vin from her bedroom. "What'sa matter? You're mad at me."

"Sure I'm mad."

"About the money."

"Peter took it and spent it and you let him get away with it. Why?"

"He must have needed it if he took it like that."

"He didn't *need* it! He spent it on his girlfriend!"

"Shhh. Rosie'll be coming back in."

"I thought *Patsy* needed it so badly."

"Shhh. Shhh. I can only do so much. Here I am an old woman, honey. I can't even get out of bed. The doctor says there's a black mass over my heart. 'Those are my sins,' I told him." Ignatia managed a laugh. "*My* sins, honey. I can't be worrying about anyone else's."

Throughout the early evening, the three of them—Rosie, Ignatia, Vin—watched the falling snow together, alternating with watching the TV. Jimmy would come to pick up Vin and his bike on his way home from the police station. But then, after they had eaten a little dinner that Rosie had prepared, Jimmy called back to say that Vin should stay there for the night.

"It's just like having Patsy here again," Ignatia told Lena on the phone from her bed. "He's sitting here in one of Ro's old sweaters and big old pairs of woolen pants. I should have some of Patsy's things here for an emergency like this with one of my grandsons. The both of them—Vin and Rosie—are all wrapped up. You should see. I'm perspiring as usual. No, I'm all right. No. I'm always all right. You know me."

At bedtime, Rosie told Vin to go to sleep in his room; the boy was chilled. Rosie said he would take the couch, though he knew he couldn't sleep. Or, out of habit, he didn't even try, and after midnight, he put on his coat and went outside. The snow had stopped. In the distance, he could hear a car stuck, trying to get free. A city sand truck went by noisily. Nothing else moved. He got out his shovel and started digging out the driveway.

He had thought of running away so many times in the past— to get away from Ignatia, this Godforsaken city, his life, yes, but also to look for his father—but he'd never known in which direction to go first. Now he knew it didn't matter.

He had begun to see how it could be: he could take the car wherever he might go. Ignatia had no need for it. She and Lena could figure a way to get around without him. He shoveled without stopping for an hour, until the driveway was completely clear.

Walking back to the house through the garden, to throw some things into a bag, he made another decision: he would introduce himself as Leo from now on—his real name, not his nickname: a lousy flower. His cousins had given him that name when he went to work as a gardener. He would never call himself that name again. It wasn't too late. He could still be like his father, a man who had trusted strangers, who wasn't afraid. Then he saw many big black birds descend. What in the world were birds doing out on a night like tonight? Crazy birds. He chased them away once, but they descended again, folded their wings and watched him, blinking their calm yellow eyes.

It began to snow again. Rosie was buried by the snow that fell all during the early morning hours; and, for an hour or two after that, until, that is, his grandson found him, Ignatia cursed Rosie, even envying him a little, believing that he had finally done what for so long he had silently intended.

# Shadow Bands

M IRA STEPPED CAREFULLY: she was being studied. She walked with exaggerated precision into her parents' kitchen. As purposefully as a blind girl, confident, unblinking, she stared straight ahead as if at some privileged vision.

Behind her, the boy—a slim brown child: Charlie Ashwell from the household next door—followed her every gesture with eyes that were huge and black and liquid, clouded with a far-off pain, one he only anticipated, maybe: a future pain. Cautiously he moved with the rigid gait of a wounded soldier, obedient hands down by his sides, dark fingers pointed. He moved as if he thought he might be in danger of knocking something over— or waking someone up—with a sudden, unexpected motion, one that might surprise even himself.

Actually, there was nothing or no one to disturb. Mira's parents were not home, and any objects of real value had been placed well out of reach of children. Not only that, but the noise of adults drunkenly shouting was coming through the wall of the row house next door. Not party sounds, not festive—anyway, this was mid-afternoon—but the sounds of desperation none too cleverly disguised, the kind that people make when they know that no one is listening to them.

In that house, identical to Mira's parents' except that it recently had *not* been made brand-new, Charlie lived with his mother and grandfather and several other family members and friends— and maybe some enemies as well. There were so many of them, in fact, that no one could accurately count them; none of their neighbors could, that is. As for the Ashwells themselves (they were sometimes called the "Awful Ashwells"), probably they just didn't bother. There certainly wasn't any need for them to count for the purpose of setting a supper table, for example, because their table never was set. Not that they even had a table. And everyone on the block, rich or poor, black or white, hoped that the Ashwells soon would take themselves and their lack of table manners elsewhere. "White Trash," they were pronounced by their neighbors—except for Charlie. Charlie *Brown* was his full nickname, given to him by the man he called "Granddaddy," because the child had a black man for a father, one, incidentally, whom he'd never seen. Clarence Wilson had been sent to jail for armed robbery six years ago, about the time of Charlie's birth. Since then, his mother'd had two more children—white— by Leslie ("Cutter") Sheppard: two more sons, Chubby (Leslie, Jr.) and Teety (Peter), with permanently dirty faces and the blazing blue eyes of every Ashwell, of the white ones, that is. And though some Ashwells eventually did leave—most notably (at least, most recently), Charlie's grandmother, Beverly Jean, who was born-again and living on a rocky farm outside Frostburg—some on the block were less hopeful than others about an imminent departure by the whole, extended Ashwell clan; after all, the family, in one form or another, had been living in the rented house going on thirty-five years.

The kitchen of Mira's parents, who'd been living in the neighborhood just six months, was an enviable place: shining copper everywhere, the latest equipment, most of it unused. Mira's parents worked late into the evening, and usually already had eaten dinner with clients by the time they taxied home.

Mira's own suppers consisted mainly of sweets—calories that were adding to the young womanliness that had begun to envelop her. She ate in front of the flickering colors of the downstairs TV. She was lonely in her new school, a new city, in her new, uncongenial, "changing" neighborhood, and had taken to befriending Charlie expressly against her parents' wishes. They objected not only to the upbringing he was being given by the nearly toothless, twenty-year-old girl (his mother) he simply called "Cathy," but because Mira was more than twice his age.

For Mira's part, she knew she ought to look for friends among her peers; knew, too, that she should be looking down on the Ashwells. Ignore them and hope they'll go away, as everyone else on the block hoped. But she didn't. She loved to play lessons with Charlie. She spent most of her free time drilling him, teaching him things. She seemed to be preparing him for something; she didn't know what.

Mira pushed up her sleeves, revealing pink chubby arms, and took the greatest care in selecting for Charlie a piece of fruit from the bowl—his reward. "Want me to cut it up for you?" She held the apple in her palm for him to admire. In her other hand she held the knife. She began to use it even before Charlie had nodded.

"What did you have for supper last night?" Mira asked, handing him a slice. She was curious about everything that went on in his household. She asked him all kinds of questions, knowing it would be rude to ask them of someone other than Charlie.

"About a hunnert bowls of raisin bran," he replied. He had taken the fruit and begun to eat it without even looking at it. Mira surreptitiously sniffed and examined any piece of food offered to her in a home other than her own.

"Did the cockroaches get in it this time?" she asked him playfully. But he answered matter-of-factly.

"Nope. They stayed in the 'frigerator."

"And how do you think they get into the refrigerator in the first place, Charlie?"

He hunched his small shoulders. "The big ones open the door for the little ones?"

"What's your favorite meal? If you could have just one thing to eat for the rest of your life, and it had to be that, what would you choose?"

"Penny cakes."

as his "father." He spoke of Cutter's proposal as if he were parting world-important knowledge.

"Well, I wish he'd hurry up and do it, then."

"Dirtball say it's dead already—that's why it smells so bad!"

"Well, is it? I thought you said you saw it."

"I did!... Or maybe it was his mother," he added more quietly, backing down.

"Maybe."

"I won't go back there no more," Charlie confided, "'cept walking on top of the cars."

"I don't blame you, but I bet Cathy doesn't like you making footprints on her car roof too much."

"She never sees me," he laughed somewhat nervously. The mention of his mother must have made him nervous. He got up and walked among the rows of vegetables, foot in front of foot carefully placed along the pathways of straw, just as Mira had shown him.

"I do it when she's not home," Charlie added. He bent down to look at a cucumber seedling. Sometimes, Mira thought, he does things just because he thinks they'll please me, like a teacher's pet, never mind what he'd really like to do. She watched him walk among the rows as cautiously as if he thought the soil were paper-thin and a step too heavy might break right through it.

"You could have a garden in your back yard, Charlie, if you cleaned it up," Mira said.

"What about the cars?"

"They could park them out on the street, like everybody else on the block."

"You park your car in your garage."

Mira had no rejoinder to this. She just watched Charlie in silence. He kept silent, too, until he added, almost to himself: "If Cathy had a garden, she'd grow things jess to step on 'em."

This remark, delivered as unbitterly as a compliment, stung Mira.

She worked long and hard on her drawing, into the evening. She enjoyed the filling in of detail on opposite sides of the picture.

"Does Cathy make them for you?"

Charlie shook his head. "Nope. Detox does." Detox was Harold Ashwell, his grandfather's brother.

After he'd eaten a slice or two more, he started back toward the dining-room table, where the playing cards were spread out. He had been able to divide them into the red and the black without trouble, but could see no difference between the club and the spade, the heart and the diamond.

Mira sat down across from him and watched his eyes work. They were two deep, round pools reflecting her whenever he glanced up to catch a helpful signal. He seemed to be able to take in a lot without moving his head. Yet, somehow, his eyes were unseeing too; he must have taught himself not to notice certain things, the better not to. Mira's eyes looked as if they did not know enough to avert themselves from anything.

"Let's play War," Charlie suggested brightly after a while—somewhat craftily, too.

"No," Mira said in her teacherly way, although she would have enjoyed a game of War. "I think we should keep trying to separate the suits."

"Thass too hard," Charlie insisted quietly.

"Never say never, Charlie. You can do it. Just look at each card. See this one?" She made the card snap. "How the sides are sharp and pointed? That's the diamond. And this one?" She snapped another. "With the rounded parts and a point at the bottom? That's the heart. Maybe we'll draw them later."

He lowered his eyes to the cards again. His obedience amazed Mira: how could he always be so good? It also made her slightly uncomfortable. He set himself to whatever task she gave him, without a sigh or a grimace or making any other kind of face, as surely Mira herself would have.

She suspected that he'd slept in his clothes: they were the same ones he'd worn yesterday. That proved nothing, but Mira liked to think that it did. Besides, Pearl, a neighbor of them both—a black woman who worked as a nurse's aide at night—had remarked to Mira's father once, and Mira had overheard, that Charlie didn't even have a bed of his own. "He must sleep hung up by a nail in the corner, like an old raggedy coat," Pearl had said. And Mira had pictured him sleeping just that way until she had asked Charlie himself and he told her that he slept with his granddaddy on the living-room couch.

Of all the Ashwells besides Charlie, it was Charlie's grandfather, Thirsty (Thurston), whom Mira saw most frequently, as he walked jauntily down the sidewalk, whistling an unrecognizable tune. He delivered packages for the liquor store on the corner in pants too short and a jacket too thin, never in a hurry. Licking his lips and adjusting his false teeth with his tongue to make a ready smile, he winked at Mira whenever they passed. She knew that he was dirty—round circles of hair had been eaten out of his scalp by something. And once she had seen him urinating without breaking his stride. That was the same day he called out to her from his porch as she left her house: "*Voulez-vous couchez avec moi ce soir?* I bet you didn't know I knew French, did you?" He came wobbly-legged down his porch steps and followed her down the sidewalk. "I know French, German, Italian, too. I was in all those places in the Navy. Shot a German *woman*. She didn't die, though."

"Don't get friendly with *any* of them," Mira's parents gently had warned her. Still she had with Charlie, and made it a point to wave or nod whenever she passed by any of the others. Thirsty, Detox, and the third brother, Burrill—all three of them, skeletally thin with gaunt, red, wrinkled faces and blue eyes that looked seared, as if they had gotten too close a look at something—waved back, cordial enough, and so did Thirsty's many sons: Daryl, Renford, Lyle, Dub, and Dirtball among them. And so did Cutter, Cathy's boyfriend, who now lived in the house as well. But Mira never said anything more to them but "Hi," though if she were walking with her parents, she did not even say that, for invariably Thirsty (and any one of the others) conveniently would let a passing car catch his eye as their paths crossed.

"Don't you know a baseball diamond?" Mira urged Charlie, seeing that, though lucky guesses had helped him a little, he still had not been able to separate the cards correctly. "A heart-shaped box of candy?" Roughly she traced the symbols on the table while Charlie shrugged, looking smaller than usual; he

was almost cowering. Then he collected himse study the cards again, but in a way that let Mir only pretending to try now.

"Okay, let's go outside in the garden and draw sighed.

Charlie followed Mira with her sketch pads and full of colored pencils out into the bright sunny recta parents' back yard. In their house he moved so still was almost theatrically careful. In their garden he relaxe They walked to the far end of the yard whose every inc was planted in rows with vegetables, herbs, and flower sat on the brick path with their backs against the garag had been warmed by the sun.

Mira began to draw the window of the Ashwells' back room on the second floor. It was broken and covered with pages of a porno magazine fastened with electrician's tape. S worked on this awhile, then decided she would draw both tha window and the window of her own bedroom, the mirror image of next door. The two houses met in a peaked roof. One half of it—the Ashwells'—stood unpainted, crumbling; and the broken window was prominent. Mira's parents' half was painted a soft blue-gray with a shade pulled down exactly one-quarter of the way and a houseplant on the windowsill.

Someday, Mira thought, she'd do a drawing of the view *from* her window *down* into the two back yards, one so different from the other. The Ashwells used their back yard as a parking lot and garbage dump. Three cars were squeezed into it, end to end. At the head of this line, up against their house, a two-man-tall pile of garbage teetered. They threw their garbage—mostly brown shopping bags full of beer cans and fast-food wrappers—out of the back bedroom window every night. A rat the size of a small dog had tunneled in and lived beneath the mound. Charlie had seen it and its burrowed cave. Mira hadn't, but both she and Charlie could smell the rodent from where they sat, on her side of the fence.

"Yuck," Mira said, holding her nose.

"Cutter say he's gonna kill it with a baseball bat upside the head," Charlie said proudly of the man he sometimes referred

Her parents were still at work; then, since it was a Friday, they were going with another couple to a movie and afterwards would get something to eat.

Charlie had gone home at once when Cathy had called him to come and eat what she'd brought him. From her side of the fence Mira had heard her say to Charlie and his two half-brothers: "And you'd better eat every fucken bite!" Cathy never even looked at Mira, ever. A tall, skinny, sallow-skinned girl with bruise-colored eyes, the missing teeth—not all of them simply fallen out, but some of them knocked out or broken off at the gumline—she grumbled and grimaced, looking down, when she and Mira passed on the sidewalk. Cathy's most frequent destination was the pay phone outside the liquor store. It was while Cathy was on the phone that Mira successfully, unobtrusively, had read the tattoo on her arm. The word she had chosen, scrawled so unprofessionally a child might have done it, was *LOVE*, in the same bruise color of her eyes.

Once, late at night, Mira had overheard Cathy and Cutter talking in the Ashwell's back yard. It sounded as if Cutter was planning to leave Cathy, and she was trying to talk him out of it. She mentioned the two sons she'd borne for him. "I hope they die!" Cutter had retorted. "Well, I'd like to see how you do out there in that big world all by yourself," Cathy had said. That seemed to end it, and Cutter evidently had stayed.

Now Cathy appeared to be pregnant again, and Mira wondered if it would be a girl this time. She didn't think Cathy would like a girl, but probably wouldn't let a little thing like the wrong-sexed child bother her much. Cathy seemed to sense an order to things, something beyond her control, and yet she was a part of it: she didn't fight it. Nothing to fight: she couldn't see it. Mira admired that in Cathy, despite everything else, including her treatment of Charlie. Mira, who felt she herself rightly belonged nowhere, even envied Cathy a little. All the Ashwells, except Charlie, truly belonged with each other.

Mira worked on her drawing until it was long past nine. She still wasn't finished when she heard noise and shouting on the street outside. It went on for quite a while, but she didn't get up to see what it was. She was used to disturbances made by the Ashwells. She half-expected Charlie to lift the mail slot in the front door—that was how he knocked—and ask to come in and tell her about it. But he didn't. And she didn't get up from the table to go look out the window until she saw the ambulance lights—red, silver, red, silver—racing around the room.

Police and police cars were everywhere, with lights and badges flashing. In the center of it all, a big black man was being bandaged, leaning up against a parked car like someone being frisked. Huge amounts of the whitest gauze were being wrapped around his middle. His head had already been wrapped in a turban of gauze by the ambulance attendants.

Several Ashwells were out on the sidewalk, shouting at the wounded man, making boxers' moves, but not getting up too close to him. Somewhere Thirsty had lost his false teeth, but still he was shouting the loudest: "I hope you die!" At this, the wounded man jerked up from the stretcher on which he had been laid and started to fight. The police restrained him, and they and the ambulance drivers eventually got him to lie back down.

Several police went into the Ashwells' house. From her window Mira could see that they all made sure to avoid a wide black pool on the sidewalk, just outside the Ashwells' gate: it glistened under the orange street lights. She watched from the window until the ambulance workers and all of the police were gone— and until it was finally, mysteriously, quiet next door. She waited a long time for Charlie to come over—to tell her what had happened. But his eyes never did appear in the rectangle of the mail slot, although several times she imagined she'd heard the squeak it made whenever he opened it.

She went to bed, and later on, heard her parents arrive home, coming in the back door from the garage. Mira didn't get up to say hello to them, or to say anything else; she pretended to be asleep. She wanted to keep wondering in the dark about the Ashwells. It wasn't the first time police had come to their door. Once, they came in the middle of the night to take Dirtball away for questioning. Mira heard them rumble up the stairs and bang on the back bedroom door, then say to him, "Be cool, now, man, be cool." The next day, no one seemed disturbed. They were all out on the front porch, as usual, drinking and laughing.

Later, Dirtball returned—a big, pimply boy of nineteen with the expression on his face of a child who thinks he's outsmarted someone—telling stories. "And you know what they gave me to eat?" he asked no one in particular, swaggering in the Ashwells' dirt patch of a front yard. "A bologna sandwich! And I said to them, 'I don't eat no bologna sandwiches!'"

The Ashwells all had been so cheerful! If the same thing had happened to either of Mira's parents or to anyone they knew, they would have been somber and busy making phone calls for days. Mira fell in and out of sleep, wondering how the Ashwells' mood would be tomorrow. She felt strangely elated, almost happy, as if she had glimpsed something of rare privilege, a thing usually hidden, one of life's secrets, direct and real. Because she never had felt this way before, and because it was for such a peculiar reason, she decided it must be a feeling she would have more often as she got more grown up. She wondered if her parents would see that she was changed. So distant, murmuring in their cavernous bedroom down the hall—they were two tall strangers in her mind's eye tonight. They would never understand that she was actually happy to be living next door to the Ashwells.

The minute she awoke the next morning, she got dressed and tiptoed downstairs. She looked again at the sidewalk, and saw exactly what last night she had only supposed: that the black was not any black at all, but the bright red blood of a person. This excited her, made her feel special for living so close to such an event, such a family who would do such a thing.

She opened the door, stepped out into the brilliant sunshine falling at an angle across the porch, and stared at the splattered side of the parked car that the man had leaned up against while the ambulance workers had dressed him. The splashes of blood he had left behind were almost artistic, free and large, like a modern painter's marks. But the wide flat puddle of red on the sidewalk, where he must have lain before the ambulance arrived, just beyond the Ashwells' gate, was redder than any paint Mira had seen on either a house or a canvas. She stared at it a long while, fascinated. When a young black man walked by and expressed to her wordlessly his own excitement and wonder at the stain—over the noise of his suitcase-sized box of blaring music—she felt proud, but knew enough to keep it inside: on her face she wore a look of ponderousness and worry.

Mothers from the projects had a different reaction, and Mira took it as a personal insult. With their laundry in wire shopping carts, and little children trailing behind them, they scuffed by with a first and then a second disgusted glance at the stain under their feet, but not a third one backwards. They did not stop. They were not fascinated or amused. And they did not look at Mira standing with her feet apart on her front porch. They kept walking, finally not seeing at all, as the wheels of their carts squealed under the weight of large households' dirty clothes.

Mira wondered after these women disapprovingly. How was it that they had come to have such a lack of simple curiosity? How was it that they deliberately chose not to see? She kept her eyes on the spot, as if it were her duty, feeling important, even enjoying herself. She still was keeping her vigil when Charlie Brown came out onto his porch.

He wore the same rumpled clothes he'd worn now for three days running. He had lint and pieces of dust caught in his matted hair. She saw that one of his eyes was blackened, and that he looked frightened and upset, but was trying not to. She was glad he chose to hide it; if he didn't, it would spoil things. She wasn't pleased with his reaction, but she also felt sorry for the boy.

"Charlie, what happened to you?" she asked gently.

"Walked into a post, wasn't looken," he said, carefully rehearsed, and even someone who didn't think they knew him would have said that he was lying. He was much more somber than she'd ever seen him before. That wouldn't be fun. She didn't like him lying to her, either, but she'd forgive him this once, under the circumstances.

"The pig won a car," he added to Mira's thoughtful silence— she was back looking at the blood.

"What pig, Charlie?" She was annoyed. Did he think she could read his mind?

"In the cartoon!" he said, his small voice straining.

"I don't watch cartoons, Charlie, you know that," she snapped. She had told him many times that most cartoons were dumb, and supposedly he had finally agreed with her.

"That's why I'm tellen you!" he shouted.

"Shh!" she warned, pointing to his door and then to her parents'. She was annoyed at the shouting and surprised at it, too.

"Then it went out," he added in a lower voice, nearly a mumble.

"What went out? The cartoon?"

He nodded at his torn sneakers, which had many knots in the laces.

"Is your electricity shut off again?" Mira sighed.

In reply Charlie just looked across at the row of town houses on the other side of the street, squinting into the yellow sun. And Mira thought of the Ashwells groping around in their dark house tonight. It was interesting when the electricity was shut off during a storm, but this was something inconvenient, not interesting at all. What could Mira do about it? Nothing. Why couldn't the Ashwells just pay their bill? They seemed to have enough money for beer and cigarettes every day, she thought self-righteously. She felt like an adult, having such an opinion. Adult-like, too, was her next idea. Poor Charlie—so what would they, she and he, do today?

"Less play lessons," Charlie said demandingly, giving his foot a little stamp. But Mira said no. He couldn't come inside when her parents were at home. They wouldn't even like it, really, if the two of them just talked together outside.

"No, let's go for a walk," she said, as if this were something they always did, although they never had before. But she'd learned long ago from her parents, indirectly, that if the tone of voice you used was confident enough, it made your idea seem that way, too. Besides, she also had this newfound importance. "Yes, we'll go for a walk. You go tell Cathy you're going somewhere with me."

"She's sleepen."

"Well, then, go tell your granddaddy."

"He's sleepen, too!"

"Well, then, come on!" And they took off together down the street.

He ran and ran in circles around her, then ran far ahead and circled back. Mira, plump, out of shape, struggled to keep up, and marvelled at Charlie's energy and strength. His upper body appeared to remain stationary, while his muscular little legs whirred beneath him. He never moved with such freedom in Mira's parents' house or yard. Nor in his own back yard or in sight of anyone in his household. She began to think she didn't know him very well after all. Even the familiar shirt he wore looked strange against this new landscape of the streets leading downtown. The shirt was red with a silver patch made of duct tape smack in the middle of the back of it, like a target, where Cathy had touched it with a cigarette. Mira kept her eye on that patch—the sun made it appear to flutter like a silver bird following him—as she struggled along, her lungs and chubby knees aching.

Passing the temperature and time on the bank sign, she shouted after him, hoping to make a number lesson out of it, but her words were lost: Charlie was too far ahead to understand them, and wouldn't come back to listen to her explain.

He tore in and out of stores, creating suspicion. She followed close behind, pulling up her socks on the run. In the drugstore he slowed, surveying the items on the shelves, while she bought a package of cough drops—this, just to show the glowering store manager that they did have some legitimate business in the place. Then Charlie ran up and told her proudly, in a loud voice, and in front of the cashier and several other customers waiting sleepily behind them in the line, that the last time he and Cathy had been here, she'd taken a chocolate bar from the display and given it to him to eat. "And she didn't pay for it or nothin'!" he beamed and then ran out the door. Mira, reddening, paid for her purchase and hurried away after him, thinking that the actions of members of his household were very often not precise and praiseworthy at all, and shouldn't be considered that way: and Charlie should know that: he should be told. But the boy was already far ahead of her up the street.

She followed him into the city park and up the grassy hill. It was the place that she had come with her class not too long ago to view an eclipse of the sun. They had been made to put their

backs to it and look at its image projected through a pinprick in
cardboard onto yet another piece of cardboard. Actually, it had
only been an *annular* eclipse. Carefully she had been taught the
distinction by Mr. Hammond, the bearded young science
teacher, who smiled too much, who wanted too much for the
students to like him, so they didn't. They did learn from him
about penumbras, shadow bands, Baily's Beads, the corona—all
in preparation for the viewing. But when the day finally came
and they looked through their cardboard contraptions, they saw
nothing even remotely spectacular. The skies had been overcast;
then they'd further darkened, but otherwise . . . nothing. Mira
was convinced that she would have seen *something* if she'd been
allowed to look at the sun directly—at least she would have
seen what there was to see of the sun that day: a large spot of
glare in the bleak, gray sky, with furious clouds racing past it.

It was here on the grassy slope that Charlie finally rested. He
threw himself down on the ground, and Mira sat, too; then she
saw that they weren't alone.

Not far off was the couple she often noticed on her way to
the school-bus stop: a tall black man in an Army fatigue jacket
and his girlfriend, who was white with red hair and always wore
skirts that swept the sidewalk. They were never not together,
and to her it looked as if they were clearly in love. The dreaminess
of their eyes was certainly something to behold. Neither would
ever hurt the other, she felt sure. Would they? Sometimes, when
she saw them walking, she had to look closely to make sure that
their eyes were open. They held hands, and each led the other
along. Probably they lived in the park; probably they were
junkies, Mira thought; but she admired them and their together-
ness anyway, at least from a distance.

"Who *was* that man at your house last night, Charlie?" she
asked, watching the man in the fatigue jacket eat popcorn from
a bag that the girl held out to him. They were sitting on a blanket
with many household items lined up on it with them. He did
look like the man who'd been hurt last night at the Ashwells'—
but it couldn't be the same person, could it? "Who was it?" she
asked again.

The boy shrugged. "I don't know." He wouldn't look at her.

Mira smirked. He really was a poor liar. "You do too know who it was, Charlie!"

"No I don't!" he said into her face.

She flinched, but persisted: "Wasn't it your father?"

"Cutter?" The boy was confused by her.

"No! Your real father!"

He was silent, chewing his lip, looking away from her again, and she saw that his unhappy mood had returned. After a while, though, she saw that a new, diverting thought had crossed his mind; he said with glee, "Cutter got him in the back with a machete!"

"Who? That guy last night? That's awful, Charlie! Is he going to be all right?"

"Cathy got a machete in the shoulder down in Virginia! She was on TV!" he bragged.

"For fighting? On the news? That's bad, Charlie. That's not good. And it's not good that she took that candy bar in the drug store, or that Detox threw a bottle through that car window, or that Dirtball . . ."

In the middle of her speech Charlie got up and started running again, this time at a group of birds feeding on the grass.

"Charlie!" Mira got up and followed after him.

Four black crows big as cats flew into the trees caw-cawing, then folded their wings and glared down at them both, while Charlie flapped his arms, jumping up and down, futilely trying to touch the lowest tree limbs.

"Charlie!"

"What?"

"Don't do that!"

"Do what?"

"Scare the birds. They aren't doing anything to you!"

In response Charlie ran and leapt at them some more, circling the wide base of the tree.

To show indifference—that is, to hide her hurt and anger—Mira turned her back on him and looked up at the sun, full-face, eyes open. She stared boldly at it as long as she could, then had to glance away with her eye sockets aching, tearing, and her vision spotty. She nearly lost her balance. When she recovered herself, she looked around for Charlie. He was over by the junkies, and so were two black girls about Mira's age.

It looked as if the girls considered themselves to be very grown up, at least to Mira. What were they all talking about? Maybe the girls were asking the junkies for drugs. They were mildly overweight, like Mira, in their new spring dresses. They must have walked over from the projects. Maybe one of them had a baby at home. Maybe both of them did. Mira felt superior to them in many ways, but she also was intimidated by them.

"Charlie!" Mira called to the boy, who stood on the edge of the group's blanket, listening to them. He ignored her, and took some popcorn from the bag held out to him. But Mira decided not to be afraid. She took the path—a dusty path; no one had meant a path to be here, but the grass had been worn by many lazy walkers over the years, and now there was a diagonal cut right through the heart of the park. She walked straight over to Charlie and the others in the group, but stayed on the path.

"Charlie, Cathy's going to be mad when she wakes up and finds out that you're gone. You better come home with me now."

But the boy just kept eating the popcorn and listening to the man whose slowly worded sentence Mira had interrupted. Everyone else but Charlie was looking at her. Finally it was one of the black girls who spoke up: "Hey, white bitch, you leave this boy alone." She had a gravelly voice and the whites of her eyes were not white at all, but yellow.

"You take care your own babies," said the other black girl. The skin of her forehead was wrinkled and so was one of her forearms—burn marks. "He not your baby, is he?"

"No!"

"Well, why you actin' like you his momma, then?" the other one said, and they both moved closer to Mira, who was still standing firm on the path.

"I'm not."

"You get outa here, bitch! Go on, go on home!" the burned girl said and picked something up off the path.

"Come on, Charlie," Mira said, frightened now, but still holding her ground. Then she saw the two girls moving, shifting directions, darting like disturbed shadows. She smelled the sweet, sharp odors of their skin. She couldn't see where Charlie was anymore. Then the burned girl's hand came up close to Mira's face as she threw some grit into Mira's eyes.

She cried out for Charlie, groping, but found only strange arms and hands that pushed and pulled her and scratched at her cheeks and pulled her hair. A blow to her stomach knocked her breath out, and she couldn't even speak. She heard them laughing as she tried to catch her breath, gasping like a drowning person. She knew she must look ridiculous. She kept sipping at the air, never getting enough. Finally, then, she could scream, but she still couldn't see. She screamed and screamed, fascinated at how good it felt to take such deep breaths, then let it all out again. She rubbed the last of the grit from her eyes, and saw that the junkies still dreamed, the girls were gone . . . and so was Charlie.

She limped home, ignoring the stares. She knew her lip was swollen and her shirt bloodied, but she didn't care. She wore these as an emblem of something.

From the head of her block she could see that her parents were busy out on the sidewalk. Her father held the garden hose and was directing it at the stain outside the Ashwells' gate. Her mother was using a stiff broom to push the water into the gutter. As Mira approached, she watched the water flow red, then pink, all along the gutter to the drain, and her stomach turned queasy. Her parents were so intent on their chore, grim-faced and offi-cious, they didn't even notice her. Later they would shriek and tear the explanations from her. But for now she sneaked up the steps of her porch, and caught sight of Charlie on his porch. He was crouched behind the wooden slats of the railing, watching her parents work. When he saw Mira, he stood and his black eyes flashed at her with hope. But the teeth of his smile looked too sharp to her now; Mira hurried past.

# ABOUT THE AUTHOR

Born in Greenwich, Connecticut, Jeanne Schinto studied at George Washington and Johns Hopkins universities. Her stories have appeared in *The Yale Review*, *New England Review/Bread Loaf Quarterly*, *The Boston Globe Sunday Magazine*, *Ontario Review*, *The Greensboro Review*, and elsewhere; and have been reprinted in several anthologies, including *The Best American Short Stories 1984* and *You Don't Know What Love Is: Contemporary American Stories*, 1987. The winner of a 1982 UNICO National Foundation Literary Award, she lives with her husband in Lawrence, Massachusetts.